# STEVIE-GIRL AND THE PHANTOM OF FOREVER

## BOOK FOUR

### ANN SWANN

5 PRINCE PUBLISHING

Published by 5 PRINCE PUBLISHING & BOOKS, LLC

PO Box 865, Arvada, CO 80001

www.5PrinceBooks.com

ISBN digital: 978-1-63112-230-9

ISBN print: 978-1-63112-231-6

STEVIE-GIRL AND THE PHANTOM OF FOREVER Copyright Ann Swann, 2019

Cover Credit: Marianne Nowicki

First Edition 2019

**Stevie-girl and The Phantom Pilot** "Just wanted you to know that my daughter needed to bring 10 things "about her that were not physical" for a class project. She brought her Tae Kwon Do trophy, a softball mitt, a few other things and your books because "they were her favorite books."
   **Elyse Sussman Salpeter**

**The Phantom Pilot** Hours of great Saturday morning cartoons, topped off, mid-day, by "American Bandstand;" the way Nestle's Quik, no matter how much you stirred it, left tasty, powdery lumps in your chocolate milk; the exuberant music of the late sixties, from Creedence to the Archies. Ann Swann brings all these cultural touchstones together in her novella The Phantom Pilot. Not only will readers of -- ahem -- a certain age appreciate the world Ann has re-created here, but kids of today will definitely identify with Stevie, the brave, vulnerable 12-year old heroine whose struggles and hopes cross generational lines. I can't wait to see what Ann has in store for us in The Phantom Student, her upcoming sequel.
   ~Amazon Review

**The Phantom Student**
   A "Must Read" for those who care about the pain and shame of school bullying. The adventures of Stevie and Jase give us an insightful look at those with Tourette Syndrome and other problems faced by those who suffer from handicaps. A good book for

public school libraries with its inspiring guidance for both students and parents. I gladly give it five stars.

*Dedicated to my sister Peggy Jean*
*I miss you, sis. I will miss you, forever.*

Note:
Although the origin of this story comes from an event in my own childhood,
the details have been fictionalized.
Let's just go with that, shall we?

## ALSO BY ANN SWANN

All For Love

Stutter Creek

Lilac Lane

Copper Lake

Remains in the Pond

Stevie-Girl and the Phantom Pilot

Stevie-Girl and the Phantom Student

Stevie-Girl and the Phantom of Crybaby Bridge

Stevie-Girl and the Phantom of Forever

# STEVIE-GIRL AND THE PHANTOM OF FOREVER

ANN SWANN

# STEVIE-GIRL AND THE PHANTOM OF FOREVER

IT WAS THE SUMMER MY GRAMPS HAD A HEART ATTACK AND I *almost lost him. You may not know me, but my name is Stevie Rae Sanders and I've been writing about myself for a while now. It's how I try to make sense of my world. Everyone is different. Everyone has a different family, and a different life. I've got it much better than a lot of kids my age. I have a wonderful grandpa who loves me very much, a best friend named Jase who is always there when I need him, and a whole town full of people I can count on when things get tough. On top of all that, I recently found out I do have a father after all, though he's been missing for years, and he even has a sister who has invited me to stay with them while I visit my dad in prison. With the addition of my aunt and her husband, my family has just expanded three-fold. I hope that's a good thing.*

*I think it is. Over the years I've discovered it's easy to lose touch with people—even those you love—because day-to-day life has a way of forcing us to move forward and keep going whether we're ready or not. Before you know it, years have crept by. It happens over and over again, even after we're gone. Yes, you read that right. I said even after we're gone. You don't believe me? Just read these letters. They're my proof. You see, Jase and I have this thing, this magnetism—that's the only way I know how to describe it—that causes us to attract spirits. We seem to attract them wherever we go.*

*It started when a small plane crashed in Jase's back pasture a couple of years ago and it hasn't ended yet. We help them, the spirits. Help them solve whatever problem is keeping them tethered to this realm. It isn't something we seek to do; it's something we have to do.*

*When I travelled to the prison to meet my father, it happened again. Only this time, I was alone. I didn't have Jase there to help me. All I had were these letters we wrote back and forth. Letters that kept me tethered to the world of my little family the same way the spirits are sometimes kept tethered to the world they once inhabited.*

June 8, 1971

Dear Jase,

Hello from Amarillo. How is my Gramps? I can't believe I left him when he needed me most. What was I thinking? Please tell me he's okay. I think I should come back home, but I never looked that far ahead. I don't even know how I am going to get home. My bus ticket was one way but for some reason I assumed it was round trip. Stupid of me. Just stupid! I feel like I'm drowning, coming apart at the seams, water seeping in everywhere. I've already been here three days and haven't even seen my dad—they can only have visitors on Sunday and I'm just—I'm lost.

Please tell me that you and Mr. Pearcy and Derol's mom are taking care of my Gramps. Tell me everything will be all right. Here I finally found my dad, well almost, and yet I feel worse than ever. Oh, Jase. I'm going to close this letter and put it out in the mailbox. The mailman will be here any moment. Sorry I'm such a downer.

Just me,
Stevie-girl

Dear Diary,

I regretted that letter almost as soon as I stuck it in the mailbox and raised the red flag. I'm not a Negative Nancy, well, not usually. At least I don't think I am. But being so far away from my Gramps, so soon after almost losing him, put me in a sour frame of mind. The fact that I'd traveled hundreds of miles on a Greyhound bus to see the dad I thought had deserted me and my late mom years earlier, well, that has just been almost too much.

The fact that I still haven't got to see him didn't help my frame of mind either. But should I burden Jase with all that? Should I make him worry, too?

I'd just about decided to go back and get my letter out of the box and tear it up, start a new one, when I spied the postman coming.

Too late.

I watched as he reached in, grabbed my letter, stuffed it in one of the pockets on his immense canvas bag, flipped down the red metal flag, and slid some envelopes inside the mail box with his other hand. It was apparent he had years of practice. He whistled a tune the whole time. Never missed a note.

Well, that's that. Now Jase will worry. Negative Nancy strikes again.

I tried turning on the TV in the hope that watching a depressing soap opera would cheer me up. It didn't work. That's when I thought about writing in this diary (which is really just a spiral notebook I brought from home). If I can't talk to anyone else, I can always talk to you, Diary.

Three days after I mailed the sad letter, I got a phone call from Jase. My words had upset him. We've been best friends for a couple of years now, ever since he caught me going in the old haunted house alone. This was back in our hometown of Cross-roads, Texas and I was upset, missing my former best friend, Karla, whose mom had moved them way out to California when Karla's dad enlisted in the service.

Jobs were scarce and even though he was older than most enlistees, he was prepared to serve our country in order to get a regular paycheck.

When he got shipped off to Vietnam, Karla freaked. We wrote each other all the time. Until then, we'd been inseparable. She lived only a block from me in Crossroads.

The day I went in the Old Taylor place, I'd gotten a depressing letter from Karla and since she and I had always talked about going in the haunted house—but never had the nerve—I decided to do it on my own. In my tiny little brain, I somehow had the notion that me being brave would help her (and her dad over there in the war) be braver, too.

Great thinking, right?

Anyhow, Jase saw me go in and he followed me, and scared me. I hit him with the loaf of bread Gramps had sent me to buy, and a friendship was born. I wound up helping him with a real phantom that turned out to be associated with the old Taylor place.

Well, I have to close this now, Diary. Writing it out has helped. A little. I'll write more later. Right now, I have to go and write to Jase.

Stevie

.  .  .

June 11th

Dear Jase,

It was good to hear your voice on the phone. Please tell your dad thanks for letting you call. I'm so sorry my letter upset you. You're right. I was about at the end of my rope. I guess I miss having you to talk to—I can't talk to my aunt. I don't really know her.

I also don't know how I would get by without you and your family.

Yep, you were right again. My gramps called me after you did. My aunt said her phone never rang so many times in one day before. I think she was only kidding.

Gramps sounded good. I'm so glad he got to go home from the hospital. He promised to call me every Wednesday so it would break up my week. But, Jase, I wasn't planning on staying here all summer. I thought a week or two. I didn't know I had to wait until Sunday to see my dad though. I guess I really don't know what I'm going to do until then.

Remember when you asked if anything weird had happened? I wasn't completely honest when I said it hadn't . . . there was something, I just don't know what it means yet. Do you know anything about prison cemeteries?

Until I got here, I didn't even know prisons had graveyards. I guess I just hadn't thought about it. I mean, who does?

Anyhow, when Aunt Sophia and Uncle Burney drove me home from the bus station we passed a sign indicating the turnoff for the prison *and* the cemetery. Jase let me tell you, I got the coldest feeling when we passed that sign. It felt as if I'd opened the freezer door at the Piggly Wiggly and just stepped right in.

But the worst part was when I turned around in my seat as we passed. There was a shape. The shape of something long, thin, and dirty black. It was so close to transparent I could almost see through it. It was a word you'll know, Jase. It was amorphous. I read that word in a book one time. Now I know what it means.

I'm not a writer like you. I don't think I'm describing it very well. It was just awful. I think it was Death, no, that's not right. Death wouldn't be hanging out at the street sign, would it? No. I think it was something even worse than death. I think it was Despair.

I took a moment and read what I'd just written.

Should I tear it up, start all over? Would Jase worry even more when he saw that about Death/Despair? He'd know it wasn't just idle worry. The two of us had seen things no one else would believe. Well, no one except my Gramps that is. He'd been there with us at the haunted schoolhouse but still, those entities had been phantoms, spirits of people who needed help crossing into the afterlife.

This thing I'd seen at the crossroads leading to the prison and the prison cemetery, it wasn't a phantom. At least I didn't think so. Every spirit or phantom we'd met before had human shapes. Human forms pretty much—except for the bear at Crybaby Bridge, but I still wasn't sure where that thing had originated—but this shape wasn't human or animal. It wasn't like anything I'd seen before.

Not at all.

Aunt Sophia called me just then. She'd fixed a great supper of chicken fried steak and mashed potatoes. Afterward we cleaned the kitchen and then sat down with Uncle Burney to watch an episode of *Bonanza*.

Everyone I knew loved that show. But now, watching it here on Uncle Burney's console TV, made me very homesick. I could picture Gramps at home in his recliner, feet up, watching it, talking to the screen the way he always did, and I wanted to be there. I felt like Dorothy. More than anything I wanted to be back in my own living room, back in my own home. Without thinking, I clicked my heels together—three times—as I sat on the end of the couch. My Keds didn't make a sound.

If Aunt Sophia or Uncle Burney noticed, they didn't say anything. Probably just thought *what a weird kid*. Or maybe they think all kids act like me. After all, they didn't have any of their own for comparison.

It was all I could do to sit through the entire episode without bawling. Even Little Joe in his green jacket couldn't cheer me. I felt I should've been home taking care of Gramps. I could picture him in his recliner, but I couldn't imagine anyone else there to look after him except for me. Besides all that, why was I even here? What had my dad ever done for me except leave?

I wondered if a few particles of Despair had entered my atmosphere when we drove past that shape. I certainly felt desperate and almost without hope.

When *Bonanza* went off, I yawned widely and wished my aunt and uncle goodnight. I didn't want to be rude and act like I didn't want to sit and visit—after all, they'd opened their home to me for as long as I wanted—but I needed to get back to my letter. I missed Jase almost as much as I missed Gramps.

Sorry for the interruption, Jase, I went to eat supper and visit with Aunt Sophia and Uncle Burney. Just forget that stuff I wrote earlier. I'm so sleepy right now I don't want to start a brand new letter.

I feel like the world's biggest jerk for not asking you about you on the phone. All we talked about were my problems. What about you? Any word on your brother, Rusty, or is he still listed as Missing In Action? How's your mom doing? Have you seen

Derol or Billy Bob since we got back from camping? It seems like that trip to Crybaby Bridge happened in someone else's life, not mine. Even with the bear and the crybaby and Nora, even with all that, I'd go back in a heartbeat if it would turn back the clock and make my Gramps well again.

So much has changed. And I'm not sure the changes are all for the better. But there I go feeling sorry for myself. Again. Sorry.

I'll change the subject. Amarillo's a big town compared to our little Crossroads. And the scenery we drove through to get here. Wow. You wouldn't believe your eyes—the huge ranches, the escarpment (I had to get that word out of the dictionary to impress you)—Jase, it looked downright otherworldly, right up your alley.

Someday I want you to see this. All I could think of as our Greyhound ate up the miles was *Gosh, I wish Jase was here to see this.* It looks just like those cowboy movies Gramps watches on TV. The wild, wild west the way it has looked for hundreds of years.

I see why it's called The Staked Plains. The land is almost empty. Sometimes—at a distance—the few trees do look like stakes sticking up out of the ground. It's so beautiful. You can see so far it's like looking into tomorrow.

Our bus driver said everyone needed to see the Palo Duro Canyon while we were nearby. I hope I get a chance to go there. The driver said this canyon is second in size only to the Grand Canyon in Arizona.

Can you believe we saw a herd of bison and an even bigger herd of pronghorn antelope? If I'd seen tipis and bronze men with bows and arrows, I wouldn't have been a bit surprised.

Okay, enough of all that. I think all your talk about words has rubbed off on me. Now, write back and tell me everything that's going on there. (And yes, I do realize how bossy that sounded, and no, I don't care.) I can't wait to hear from you, especially after you see my Gramps. He says he's good, but I know you'll tell me the truth.

Just me,
Stevie-girl

P.S. Have you written any new stories? I'm going to the library tomorrow, but my aunt and uncle will both be at work. I have to learn how to take the city bus. Not like Crossroads where I could just jump on my bike and pedal over. Wish me luck. I will probably need it.

*June 13*

*Dear Stevie,*

*It was so great to get your letter. By the time you get this reply, you will have seen your dad. I hope it went well. My mom includes you in her prayers every night. I do, too, (you, and Rusty, of course. And your Gramps). I don't think I've ever prayed so much in my entire life—sorta reminds me of what your aunt said about her phone ringing so often.*

*Now that business about the black shape at the sign leading to the prison is really freaky. You and I have seen lots of odd things, but that, Stevie, that sounds different. Kind of evil. It really worries me. Should I come and get you? I can take the bus. Let me know, you hear?*

*Other than that, the scenery sounds fantastic.*

*Maybe someday you will take me to the Llano Estacado—isn't that the name of that famous escarpment?—and to the Palo Duro Canyon as well.*

*I can't wait to hear all about your visit with your dad. Maybe after you see him you will want to come home. Your Gramps said he has already given your aunt the money for your return ticket. And no, he's not lying. He really is doing well. The church ladies cook for him all the time. I think Widow Conner is down there even more than at the church. He's in good hands. Mr. Pearcy looks in on him every day, too. You can stop worrying. I promise.*

*No. There isn't any news about Rusty, but Mom says even when he is found, it may take a while to notify us because the war in Vietnam is so chaotic.*

*Billy Bob was over just yesterday. We took turns riding Buddy around the pasture and down the long lane. Derol said he was going to come over when he gets back from camp. Remember, the mayor got him into that week long camp in Dallas for kids with Tourette's? He was so excited. He said his dad is coming in at the end of summer since he finally sold their house in Manila.*

*He told me to tell you to come and play basketball with him and his dad when he gets here. And me, too, of course, but he told me to tell you about it three times. I think he misses you almost as much as I do.*

*I am working on a new story. It's about a girl who gets chased by a bear—an intergalactic bear-like creature, that is. It chases her from planet to planet throughout the galaxy. They finally wind up on Mars at the same time her spaceship has a solar-panel malfunction. That's where they have the showdown with laser guns and a new cognitive weapon, which I can't describe without spoiling the ending. Just believe me when I tell you it isn't what you'd expect. I'll send you the story as soon as I'm done—if you're not home by then. But I bet you will be. I hope you will be.*

*How was the trip to the library? Tell me what you checked out. I'm reading* Fahrenheit 451 *by Ray Bradbury. It's really strange and disturbing, but my mom said to tell you to read another book by him called* Dandelion Wine. *She said it reminds her of you. She also told me she really enjoyed having you along on our camping trip, sharing the tent with you even though you yell in your sleep sometimes. Anything you want to tell me about, Stevie-girl?*

*Ok, I have to go now. I'm heading down to Skinny's Service Station to see about a job. If I can pump gas over the summer and save up those paychecks plus add it to what Mr. Pearcy pays me for mowing the lawn, I might have enough for a down payment on a car by the time I get my license —if I can get that hardship license—when I turn fifteen. I can't wait. Independence. Things will be so much different.*

*But you'll be home by then, right? By the way, did you see the moon last night? It was only a sliver. A fingernail moon . . . a ghost's smile. Did you see*

*it? I thought you might be looking at it. I hoped you*
*were anyway.*
*Write me soon,*
*Your Jase*

The letter from Jase was just what I needed. I hadn't waited for him to reply before I started writing one, though, I just went back to the one I'd already started and added the date I was going to mail it. I found myself writing to Jase every night, just like in my diary. I can't help it. I have so much to tell him . . .

June 16th
    Dear Jase,
    I saw him. Big Steve. When the guard led us (Aunt Sophia and me) into the fenced off visitation area, he stood up from a picnic table and opened his arms.
    Jase, I knew it was him immediately. I didn't so much recognize him as I just somehow *knew*. And then I ran. I ran to my dad and let him wrap me up inside his arms and we hugged and hugged. It's as if we were both just waiting on the other one to stop. I was sort of embarrassed when we finally backed away. It was good, though. I wasn't so nervous after that.
    The ride over there was agony. Especially when we approached the prison and it was all silver spiky fencing and wide gray buildings. It seemed like we'd never get there. That road was so long. It may have seemed longer because I found myself watching for the black see-through shape I'd seen before. I wasn't disappointed when I never saw it. Confused, yes. Disappointed, no. It sort of reminded me of the spooky skull I

saw in the Piggly Wiggly back home that time—right before I went in the old Taylor house.

It also made me wonder if the black shape was a harbinger of things to come. Isn't that what you called the skull, a harbinger? I think I called it an omen, a sign. But I like your word better.

Anyway, after we turned on the long road going past the spiky fence, I began to feel like I was going to puke or pass out, or both. But I didn't. Although going through those huge gates with the guard towers on each side, and then having to put all our belongings in a wire basket so the guy at the desk could inspect them . . . that felt like something out of a book or a movie. It just didn't seem real. (Still no black shadow, though, thank God.)

Finally, we got to see him. And Jase, even though I knew it was him right away, Big Steve is nothing like I remembered. Do you think I changed him in my mind, I mean in my memories? You're the writer—are memories really that subjective? I recall Mrs. Flint saying that one time—what were we reading that made her say that? Was it *The Outsiders*? I really loved that book—and that teacher. We had a lot of fun dressing you up like Pony Boy for Halloween, didn't we?

Anyhow, he isn't really that big, my dad. Not like I thought, well, not really. He's tall, but kind of thin. And he has gray at his temples, like Vincent Price. But he doesn't look like Vincent Price, not at all. Don't get that impression. You know who he looks like? He looks like me. A tall, thin, whip-cord version of me. It's weird.

My aunt took a picture of the two of us together. She said when she takes up the rest of the exposures on that roll of film she will get them developed and make copies for me. I took one of her and my dad together, too. Hard to believe they are siblings. She is small and blonde, he is tall and brown/gray.

Now if only my mom was here to be in the photos. That would be righteous. But, of course, she was on her way here when she died. I can say that a lot easier on paper than I can in person.

Is that how writing is for you? Do you say things in your stories that you can't say in real life? Just curious. You don't have to tell me if you don't want to.

By the way, I *was* looking at that moon, but we had some clouds and it was only visible for a few minutes and then the sky pulled the cloud-blanket over it again. It makes me feel better knowing we're looking at the same thing. Do you know how to find the North Star using the Big Dipper as a reference? We could look for it each night. Finding north. I like the sound of that. Especially since I'm so far north of where you are.

Tell your Mom I'm going to get *Dandelion Wine* on my next trip to the library. And I'll get *Fahrenheit 451*, too. Have you read *The Martian Chronicles*? I feel certain you have, it looks like your sort of book, it is a book of short stories, after all.

I'm going to read it, too. But right now, I'm reading *Anne of Green Gables*. It belonged to my mom. I always meant to read it but I would pick it up and then put it back down. It's like I was afraid to open it for some reason. I don't know why. Sort of like going in the old Taylor place because Karla and I never got up the nerve. Can you believe I thought to bring the book with me? I felt like I had to bring something from Mom on this trip.

Being here, away from everything I know, is making me sort of sad, but it's giving me more nerve than ever. I'm reading the book. I'm taking the bus all by myself, and I'm learning to be by myself—a lot—while my aunt and uncle are at work.

I can't wait to see my dad again next week. After that, I may tell them I'm ready to come home. We'll see.

Please write soon, Just me,

Stevie-girl

P.S. *A ghost's smile?* You're right. That's exactly how it looked.

After I wrote Jase, I figured I'd better pen a letter to Gramps, too. Not that I didn't want to, I was dying to tell him about my visit to the prison. It was just easier to talk to Jase; after all, Gramps is the one who had kept Big Steve a secret from me all these years. But I don't hold that against him, not really. I was mad at first, but I couldn't stay mad with him in the hospital, practically on his deathbed. And now, well, I don't want to write and have him hear how homesick I am.

I never want to disappoint my Gramps. Ever. That's why I try to be careful with my words, I mean in my letters. He needs to worry about getting well. He doesn't need to be worrying about how I'm getting along.

It's just easier to be truthful with Jase. I guess that's what friends are for.

June 18
    Dear Gramps,
    It was good to talk to you the other day. How are you feeling now? Jase says you are doing well—I can't wait to see you—I feel like I should be there.
    Yes, I saw Big Steve. He is tall and skinny and has graying brown hair. I showed him pictures of you and me and Gran. Then I pulled out a picture of Mom and he started crying and held it to his chest and didn't give it back.
    I let him keep it for now. I'll see him again next week. I can't decide whether to ask for it back or not. He also kept the picture of the three of us, as well as my latest school picture. He said he was going to put them on his wall. I wonder what we will look

like, on the wall of a prison cell? I guess I won't ask him. It seems weird, thinking of things like that.

He showed me a small picture of Mama and me that he said he used to keep in his wallet—when he was in the "real world" as he calls it. Now they don't let them have wallets, so it is on his wall, too. I could see the remnants of the Scotch tape on the edge of the photo. I guess he will tape them all.

I feel bad for him, Gramps. I know what he did was wrong.

He told me the whole story of what happened.

He said he was drinking in a bar when some guy made him mad. You probably already know this, Gramps, but he said he hit that man. Knocked him unconscious. The bartender called the police and they came to arrest Big Steve, but he said that's when he got in his car and took off. Driving drunk. Running from the cops. No wonder they arrested him. He said they might not have sent him to prison if he hadn't fled.

He said the other guy was all right, but when he came to he pressed assault charges. I never knew about that part, Gramps. Did you?

Anyhow, to me he seems like a normal man—not a monster or an alien like I had imagined. Thank you for saving those letters for me. I always thought he just didn't want us—me and Mom, but especially me. Now I know different. He really did write me every year on my birthday and Christmas and some-times in between. Anyhow, I just wanted you to know I'm really glad you saved the letters. I'm just sorry it took a heart attack for me to get to read them.

Enough of that. New topic.

Aunt Sophia is very nice, but her and Uncle Burney work all the time. It's neat that she loves her job though. She works for the city. I think she is someone's secretary or something (I hate to ask too much. I don't want to seem nosy.)

As for me, I think I've watched more TV since I've been

here than I have in my entire life. It's strange, though. Even my favorite shows like *American Bandstand* seem different here. It makes me so homesick when it comes on. Is it possible to miss a living room, a couch?

I've read a ton of library books, too (nothing new there). Did you know a doctor has to go to college for EIGHT years? I'm thinking about being a doctor. I want to help people who are hurting. Or have a heart attack.

Do you think I'm smart enough to be a doctor, Gramps? Big Steve said "definitely," but then he doesn't really know me. He's just being kind, I bet.

It was nice visiting with him. But it's pretty strange with all those men in their uniforms and all the families milling around the yard with us. It wasn't bad though. We got to sit outside in a shady area with picnic tables and everything. I think this place is only for men with kids who come to visit. He said there are three levels at the prison and he is in the minimum-security level. If not, I would have to visit him behind a glass partition.

Well, anyhow, I look forward to seeing him again, soon. I intend to get up my nerve and ask him if he is ever going to get out of there. Do you think I should, or shouldn't? I don't want to make him feel worse than he already does, but I think it might be neat to have him as a father again. Maybe. What do you think about that, would he go back to drinking, do you suppose?

I guess I've asked enough questions. Tell me what's going on in Crossroads. Jase said the Widow Conner is enjoying taking care of you. Is she a good cook? Tell Mr. Pearcy hello from me when you see him again.

Take care of yourself and I will see you soon I hope.

Love you lots,

Stevie-girl

P.S. I can't wait to get home. Did you already give Aunt Sophia money for my return ticket?

I folded the letter and slipped it into an envelope. Aunt Sophia had given me my very own unlined paper, a box of envelopes, and a book of stamps. It made me wonder if she knew how homesick I felt.

As I licked the envelope to seal it, a shadow crossed the window. It was the big picture window opposite the coffee table where I sat on the floor with my back against the sofa.

Must have been a bird, I thought. A big one. The shape of the wing soaring past had given me a start. It reminded me of Jase's short story about the Phantom Pilot whose small plane had soared over his house that night, just before it crashed in the field behind their barn.

I shivered and stood, careful not to bark my shins on the corners as I made my way around the coffee table to the window.

Peering out, one hand shading my eyes against the strong sunlight, I spied the bird sitting on the topmost branch of a fruitless mulberry tree at the corner of the yard. Wow. I'd never seen a bird with tail feathers that actually cascaded down below the branch like a fancy-lady's fan. It looked almost like a cartoon with its speckled brown coloring and royal green neck and red crest.

In a burst of insight, I realized I was looking at my very first pheasant. I'd never seen one in real life before, only in pictures.

As I watched, the bird took flight again. I told myself I could hear the rush of its wings as it lifted off, but of course that was impossible. It was across the yard and I was standing behind a thick pane of glass.

But hear it, I could.

And the sound grew louder. And louder.

And even louder until it enveloped the whole noonday room causing me to hunker down and squeeze my eyes shut and cover my head with my arms.

*Bang!*

Something hit the glass where I'd been standing a split second earlier.

My eyes flew open as the huge bird wheeled away, unscathed.

The pane shivered the way I'd done only moments earlier. And then a crack appeared. It started from the center of the window and began to unravel its way across the glass in a strange pattern.

Right before my eyes, the image of the pheasant took shape.

My heart fluttered as if it, too, had wings. I could hear the minute sound of the glass fracturing as the picture appeared. I wanted to close my eyes again, but I couldn't look away. All at once, a feeling stole over me. A feeling of stillness, of waiting.

I realized the window was about to burst. As soon as the last feather was formed, I imagined the glass exploding inward, right into the house, into my eyes, into my disbelieving brain.

My feet began to back away.

The crackling sound grew louder. The image became sharper, clearer.

The coffee table met the backs of my knees.

And I scooted it across the floor until it came up against the sofa.

I nearly fell, but then three things occurred in unison. The phone rang, momentarily grabbing my attention. The window shattered.

The sparkling glass pheasant soared into the sunlight.

I ignored the phone and ran to watch the flight of the fantastical bird.

All I saw were trails of feathers glittering in the air like long thin prisms that suddenly began to shed sparkles. And then the sparkles turned to black specks floating down through the air. It reminded me of the formless black shape somehow.

The phone rang and rang.

I looked toward it, the sound so insistent it seemed in danger of yanking itself off the wall. I ran to pluck off the receiver before that could happen. As I put it to my ear, it occurred to me that the window had not imploded. No glass fragments had flown through the air, no shards shimmered on the floor, or in my hair.

The shattering had been just an illusion.

I pressed the phone receiver to my ear. "Hello?" I could barely squeak out the word.

"Help me . . ." a breathy voice whispered.

I yanked the receiver away and stared at it in shock. My eyes were drawn back to the whole, unbroken, window. A blackish shape fluttered at the edge of my vision. Despair wanted my attention. Or was it the pheasant? Maybe the two things had encountered each other. Maybe they were at war.

On the phone, a voice waited. I knew it was the voice of a phantom.

I forced myself to bring the mustard-colored receiver back to my ear. "How?" I asked. "How can I help?"

No one answered. All I heard was the faint sound of wings beating the air.

Then nothing.

I glanced from the window to the phone and back again. Someone needed help. Of course they did. The whole cracked-glass-pheasant had been nothing but some phantom's attempt at communication. But what could it mean? With the Phantom Pilot—Mr. Gilpin—there had been words cut from newspapers.

He'd been pretty clear on what he needed from us. But a bird? What could a beautiful bird possibly represent? I replaced the receiver on the wall base and walked back to the adjoining living room. I couldn't wait to tell Jase what happened. I needed his input more than ever.

I straightened the coffee table and picked up my letter that had fallen to the floor. I carefully tore a stamp out of the tiny book, licked the back, and affixed it to the corner of the letter.

When I could no longer avoid it, I let myself approach the plate glass window.

The large green leaves on the mulberry tree swayed in a slight breeze. A few birds flitted about the branches of the majestic old tree. But they were small sparrows and finches. The largest was a noisy mockingbird who seemed inordinately proud of her new song.

My hands went to the glass. It was smooth and warm from the strong Texas sun. I traced what might have been the shape of a large bird, but only from recent memory. There was absolutely nothing marring the surface of the pane.

I inhaled shakily.

Thank God it didn't really break, I thought. What would I have told Aunt Sophia, Uncle Burney? They would have thought I was crazy, Looney Tunes. They would have sent me straight home on the next bus.

Not for the first time, I wished I could call Jase on the phone, but long distance charges would have to be paid. And it wasn't my phone. Instead, I took out another sheet of paper and began a new letter. I knew if I didn't get it down on paper immediately, I would begin to forget the details.

I glanced at the clock. The postman would be coming soon. I might not be able to finish this page before he came to pick up the outgoing mail. Besides, I'd already put the stamp on the other envelope. I couldn't open that one and waste a stamp on a new one. This letter would just be the start of next week's news. Unless I could find some Scotch tape in Aunt Sophia's junk drawer.

I jumped up and ran to the kitchen, pulled open the drawer where all the odds and ends lived, and rummaged through the doodads. If there was tape, I could open my already-stamped envelope with a butter knife, slip the new page inside, and then tape it shut. That way I wouldn't have to use another precious stamp.

*Voila!* There it was, the little clear plastic dispenser with the green paper insert. Scotch tape.

I hurried back to the coffee table, jotted down the rest of the unbelievable pheasant incident for Jase, ran back to the kitchen for a butter knife, slid it under the flap (it was more difficult to open than I'd thought it would be, but I finally got it with only a few rips), then I stuck the new page inside, and sealed it up with a couple of pieces of clear tape.

That's when I heard the whistling.

The postman always seemed jolly. A little on the stout side, with good sturdy walking shoes and what I suspected was a permanent indentation in his left shoulder (from carrying the heavy canvas bag full of letters), he always had a smile on his face when he saw me waiting beside the mailbox at the edge of the yard.

"Good afternoon, young lady." His voice was deep and friendly. "Beautiful day, isn't it?"

I smiled and glanced up at the clear sky and bright sun. "It sure is." I watched his hand delve into the outside pocket on the big bag. Anything in there for me, Stevie Rae Sanders?"

He pulled out three or four envelopes and a colorful advertisement. "Sorry. Not today." He handed me the mail. "Staying here with your aunt and uncle?"

I nodded. Surprised he knew who I was.

He must have seen the look on my face. "Your aunt told me you might be getting mail here for a while." He touched the edge of his billed cap in a mock salute. "Welcome to the neighborhood, Stevie Sanders. I hope you enjoy your stay."

I grinned and echoed his salute. "Why thank you, kind sir." I tried to see the name on his uniform shirt, but his raised arm covered it.

"Call me Clancy," he said. "Everyone does."

Lowering my hand, I nodded. But I doubted I could call him Clancy. I hadn't been raised to call adults by their first name. "Thank you." I turned to go back to the house. "And keep your eye out for a pheasant flying around." I glanced toward the unbroken picture window. "I thought I saw one earlier."

That stopped him in his tracks for a moment. I saw him raise the bill of his cap as he scanned the treetops. Oh, brother. Why did I say that? Now he probably thinks I've lost my marbles.

I hurried up the porch steps and back into the quiet house. Desperate, I thought. I'm just desperate to talk to people. Not used to being alone all the time.

In the kitchen, I popped ice cubes from the plastic tray and made myself a glass of iced tea. Then I tuned the radio to the local Top 40 station and took my tea onto the back patio to think about what the appearance of the pheasant could mean.

Now that the incident was behind me, I couldn't believe I was so worried about wasting a stamp when only moments before I'd been certain I was about to be decapitated by flying glass. Once again, I chalked it up to desperation. Desperation and just flat not thinking straight.

I sipped the sweet tea.

What next, I thought. What will happen next? Once these things start, they don't usually just stop. I (or usually, we) have to bring them to a close by finding the phantom and helping them solve the mystery of why they are still, well, still haunting the earth.


**June 19**

   *Dear Stevie,*

   *What the heck? A pheasant? A phantom pheasant? C'mon! That's the strangest thing I've ever heard. Well, maybe not the absolute strangest when I think back on flying records, gray blobs of rain, and magic newspaper words, but still . . . the glass wasn't broken but the image appeared? And you say the black shape hovered around, too? Man. I wish I had been there to see that. What do you think, should I come up?*

   *It sounds like you are doing well all things considered. Are you sure I don't need to come? Please, let me know if I need to hop a bus . . .*

   *Changing topics.*

   *Did you like going to the library all by yourself ? I'm reading a lot, too. (But probably not as much as you.) I got the job at Skinny's and I work there every night except Sunday when they are closed. I work from 4:00 to 10:00 with a half-hour off for supper. But I'm going to tell Skinny I can eat a sandwich there. It seems like a waste to take a half-hour off if I don't need to. I just sit in the back and read and eat anyhow.*

   *I'm making plenty of money, Stevie. By the end of summer I will have enough for a down payment.*

*I've got my eye on an El Camino. It's cherry red with a white vinyl top. I drove it in the parking lot of the Piggly Wiggly last night. It belongs to Cob Hoskins but he's selling it because he wants a new pickup truck. My dad says he'll co-sign for a loan if I save the down payment. He says it will be good for me to learn how to handle monthly payments— although it seems like I might even have enough to pay it off completely, if I save every penny.*

*No more riding bikes for us, Stevie-girl. This fall, I'll be able to drive us to school. Provided I get the hardship license, that is.*

*Skinny also says I can keep working after school starts, but a few less hours—maybe six to nine or something like that. I'm learning a lot at the station. At least I'll be able to take care of my car when I get it.*

*I can't wait until you get home.*

*You crack me up, Stevie-girl, talking about having more nerve now. Have you forgotten the bear, and the phantom pilot, and the phantom student? And even the little-crybaby-ghost? Have you forgotten the reason I followed you in the old Taylor Mansion was because you went in first? Alone?*

*Stevie-girl, you've always had more nerve than any of my guy friends. I'm going to rename you Stevie-the-Brave. It sounds like a name fit for a space-cadet-knight, doesn't it? Oh, man. That gives me an idea for a story about Knights on Mars featuring Stevie-the-Brave. Has a pretty cool ring to it, don't you think? Okay, maybe it's a little childish but hey, it's just fiction, right?*

*Have you heard any good music lately? For some reason I keep listening to that song by Stevie Wonder, "Signed, Sealed, Delivered, I'm Yours." Do you know that song? Have you got a music store nearby? I don't know exactly how big that town is, but I'll bet it's really big if they have a city bus route. Shoot, almost every town is big compared to Crossroads.*

*Well, it's time for me to go to work. I can't get used to saying that. But I like it. I feel grown up saying it. I wouldn't tell anyone else that, but I know you will understand. Here's the funny part, though. It's time for me to go to work, so I have to get on my bike and ride there. Isn't that a hoot?*

*By the way, I do know how to find the North Star using the Big Dipper. Now, I go out and say hello to it every night. I hope you do, too.*

*Write me soon, Stevie-girl,*

*Your Jase*


June 23

Dear Jase,

No. As much as I want you to, you don't need to come. Wait until I tell you what I found out about the pheasant.

I'll start at the beginning.

You know all those books we've been talking about? Big Steve has read every one. He reads all the time. They have a prison library, but he says he gets most of his books from a mail order catalog. He says it looks sort of like a newspaper and they can order as long as they pay in advance. He said after he reads them he donates them to the prison so other guys can enjoy them, too.

Did you know they get paid for working in prison? Not much, only 12¢ an hour, but he says he's saving it all up for me—he has an account or something—he says the only thing he spends money on is books and personal stuff like toothpaste. Guess that's where I get my love of reading. I hope I don't inherit his bad stuff, too. Like drinking. Some people up here say it's a disease, drinking too much, becoming an alcoholic. Do you think that's true?

I also want to know how drinking relates to violence. I never knew my dad to be violent, not ever, but I found out the whole story about how he wound up in here. I'll tell it to you in person when I see you. I'm still trying to process it all myself.

I'm going to do some research on the topic of alcoholism when I get a chance. It's just one more thing to think about.

By the way, I'm so glad you love working at Skinny's. Not only will you be able to afford that El Camino, but it will also keep you out of trouble until school starts again. Just kidding.

Tell your mom I loved *Dandelion Wine*. It made me want to time-travel back to that period Mr. Bradbury described so well. Wouldn't it be cool to launch a few fire-balloons? Wow.

But it also made me afraid to go outside after dark. I can't help but wonder if The Lonely One might be watching me.

Big Steve had my aunt buy me a copy of *A Wrinkle in Time*, that science fiction book by Madeline L'Engle. I've seen it at the library so many times, and almost picked it up, but like my mom's book, I just never did.

As soon as I started reading, I couldn't put it down. Jase, it's so odd. The story is about a girl who has to find and rescue her missing father. There's also a kindly aunt called "Aunt Beast" who is a really strange looking alien (I'll never be able to think of my aunt as anything else, now), and there's the idea—I think it's sort of like the theme (wouldn't Mrs. Flint be proud to hear me say that?)—that sometimes kids have to take responsibility for themselves because parents just can't fix everything.

Do you think my dad read it and knew all these parallels before he got it for me? Oh, there's also a tall, handsome, older boy the girl falls for. Big Steve couldn't have known about *that* parallel even though I did tell him all about *you*. Haha.

Okay enough of that. Tell me what's going on in your life. Tell me about home. I miss you and everyone there. I'm sending all my love.

Just me,

Stevie-girl

I ended the letter to Jase and simply sat for a while. I knew in my heart that he already realized how I felt about him. But we'd never actually said it before. Until now, we hadn't written each other because we'd been together all the time. He was my best friend. I expected he always would be. We had been through so much together with the phantom stuff and his brother going missing, but for some reason it felt different now. Maybe that old saying really is true; maybe absence really does make the heart grow fonder.

As if that's even possible.

I folded the letter and stuffed it in the envelope then went to check the window for pheasants or postmen named Clancy, whichever came first.

I laughed at my own private joke. Being alone all the time was hard. Talking to myself inside my own head was becoming second nature. If I started talking aloud, I guess I'd know it was time to go home. I was pretty sure it wouldn't be long before that happened.

Looking out the window made me realize being cooped up inside might be part of my problem. I never stayed indoors back home.

I put the stamp on the letter and took it out to the mailbox then I went exploring. My aunt had said it was okay to look around as long as I left a note to tell her where I was going in case she got off work early. But I didn't intend to go off the block today. I just wanted some fresh air even it was hot enough to scorch my lungs every time I inhaled. Besides, Clancy would be here any time now. Maybe there would be a letter from Gramps.

*June 24th*

*Dear Stevie,*

*I miss you girl. But I'm doing fine, just fine. Gettin' fat from all the cakes and brownies and rhubarb pie Widow Conner keeps bringing me.*

*Hope you can read this old henscratch, I haven't written a letter in a long, long time.*

*Glad to hear you got to see Big Steve. I guess you know I'm having a little trouble forgiving him for what happened to your mom. I blame him for leaving you two in the lurch way back when. And then when he got drunk and knocked that guy out and then topped it all off by running from the cops. It just confirmed my worst opinion of him.*

*He shouldn't have done all that—but I keep reminding myself that no one is perfect. I know it isn't his fault your mom got in that wreck. But she was my only daughter. I hope you never have to understand that bitter feeling.*

*It's good that you're getting to know him a little bit. I know you always wondered about him. I never knew you thought he stayed away because he didn't want you. That makes me feel bad. I guess I assumed you thought he was dead and gone, and tell-you-the-truth, I was okay with that. Guess I'm not perfect either.*

*So, has the big city got its grip on you, girl? Get used to it. You'll be going off to college in a few years and this will help you know that you can handle it. Riding a bus around town is a good start. Just don't trust everyone you meet. Use that noggin and always pay attention to your instincts. Of course, I think you're smart enough to be a doctor. You're the smartest kid I know. And you have common sense, too. That's something you can't get out of any book. You just keep on believing in yourself and I'll see to it you become a doctor or whatever you want to be.*

*I love you, Stevie-girl. And yes, I've already given Sophia the money to get you home. I sent it to her through Western Union as soon as I got out of the hospital. I miss you more than anything, but I'm doing all right. Don't worry. I'll see you when you're ready.*

*Gramps*

July 5th

Dear Jase,

Happy Late Fourth of July!

I can tell you are having a great summer and that makes me happy. I haven't got up the nerve (ha ha) to try and find the music store yet. It's downtown and I'm sort of saving my money anyhow. But I might go if I get too bored. I keep thinking I will be coming home soon, but then I think I'll visit Big Steve just once more before I go because who knows when I'll ever come back. Does that make sense? I hope it does. Now that I've seen him, I'm not so homesick.

Hey, speaking of music, I love that new song by James Taylor, "You've Got a Friend." Do you like it? Oh, and how about that one by Paul Revere and the Raiders, "Indian Reservation." It's different, isn't it? Every time it comes on the kitchen radio I have to run and turn it up. I love that kitchen radio. Aunt Sophia has it on the windowsill and when it rains, or the wind blows hard, the music fades in and out and the announcer's voice squawks like an old goose.

It reminds me of home. Reminds me of Gran. She loved her radio on the windowsill, too. On cloudy days, when this one squawks and slips off the station, I'd swear I can almost see Gran standing at the sink in her soft cotton apron and comfy old slippers. It's like she's here in the gaps. I miss her as much now as when I lost her four years ago. I just don't know how to let go, it seems.

Okay, I've put it off as long as I can. What did you do for July 4th? I don't like thinking about the parade. It's the first time I've missed it since I first moved to Crossroads. Was it great? You know, I should have been there marching in the band. I really should—but I know I'll be home soon. This is only one summer out of all of my summers. That's what I keep telling myself anyhow.

I had a very strange July 4th here. Since it was Sunday, we got to go and visit Big Steve. That was about as different as you can imagine. But here's something even stranger than spending Independence Day at a prison, and not just the (what's that word you like so much?) the irony of it—being behind bars on Independence Day—nope, the really strange part was being sent to the prison cemetery to deliver a message.

Talk to you soon,

Just me,

Stevie

P.S. "Who'll Stop the Rain" might be my favorite song of all time (except for "Crimson & Clover" and "Bobby McGee" of course).

I got Jase's letter ready to mail. I tried my best to be positive and to let him know how much I missed him without letting on how much I *really* missed him. I knew I left him hanging about going to the prison cemetery, but that's what he always did in his stories . . . wrote cliffhangers. So in away, it's his own fault. At least that's what I will tell him. In reality he'll know it's just because I love to tease him. It's the way we communicate. Has been since I first whacked him with a loaf of bread in the old haunted Taylor Mansion.

Tomorrow I will have to write a letter to my Gramps. Even though his last letter was really serious, in real life he's quite a teaser. In fact, he's the best teaser in the world. Sometimes I can't even tell the difference.

July 6th

Dear Gramps,

Thanks for the letter. I'm glad everyone is taking such good care of you. Tell Widow Conner I'll be home soon to take care of you myself.

Big Steve wrote you a letter and I'm enclosing it with mine. He said if you don't want to read it that's okay. What he said is that he got sober the hard way and that he will never forgive himself for leaving Mom and me. He also says he holds himself accountable for her death because he knows she would not have been on that highway if she hadn't been looking for him.

I told him I don't blame him, that I'm not mad at him. I don't know if that was the right thing to do, but when I looked in his eyes—just like mine but set deep down in a whole nest of crinkles—I can see that he does feel responsible. He says it still keeps him awake at night, wishing he'd never left the house after that argument. I think that's enough punishment for anyone. I hope you understand and aren't mad at me.

Aunt Sophia also told me how sorry she was that she'd told Mom where to find Big Steve. But I just pshawed her the way you taught me. I mean, good grief, no one could know she would get in a wreck that way. Why feel guilty?

Now, tell me about the July 4th fireworks and parade. I'll bet the mayor drove his big red convertible, didn't he? Did he throw tons of candy like always? What was the grand finale, did they make a red, white, and blue fireworks flag like last year? I'm sorry I missed it. But I'll be there for the next one.

Write me when you can. I love you, too. Very much! Stevie-girl

After I mailed the letter to Gramps, I got my newest library book and curled up in Aunt Sophia's reading chair. I loved the tall gooseneck lamp that curved down over it. Aunt Sophia liked reading, too. She had a whole bookshelf full of Harlequin romance novels.

I loved reading, but I was also getting addicted to some of the daytime TV shows like *Let's Make a Deal* and even began to look forward to some of the soaps like *The Days of Our Lives*. I guess you could say I was settling in. Making a new life for myself. Oh, I knew it was temporary, but having Big Steve close by made a difference. I could hardly believe it myself, but I knew it was true. I could feel it. Did having a new mystery to solve help? I think it did.

**July 9th**

*Dang it, Stevie!*

*I can't believe you left me hanging like that! What do you mean you had to deliver a message to the prison graveyard? Tell me all about it. Who sent you there? Was your Aunt with you, or did you go alone? Jeez-Louise, did you see the black shape-stuff? Or the pheasant?*

*I'll get you back for making me wonder all these days. How I wish I could pick up the phone and call you anytime I want, but I can't—Mom and Dad are worrying about money for some reason. I don't know what's going on, Dad seems to be having some sort of financial difficulty or something.*

*Anyhow, I'll get my first paycheck next week and I'm going to open a bank account. I'll have both checking and savings accounts. Can you believe I'll be able to write a check? I'm saving for that down payment, but first I will call you. And I will give Dad the money for the call so he can't say anything. As for the parade—it was okay. But not the same without you. When the band turned the corner downtown, I couldn't even watch. I ran out with Billy Bob and grabbed a bunch of candy when the mayor threw it, but I felt stupid, like a little kid.*

*Like on Halloween when you all of a sudden realize you're too big to trick-or-treat anymore.*

*If you were there, it might've been different. I wouldn't have felt so self-conscious. After all, you really are just a little kid. Haha. But yeah, it was a blast having you dress me up like Pony Boy last Halloween—you can do that anytime—of course the haunted schoolhouse was a serious bonus, too, wasn't it? I get shivers just remembering it.*

*The fireworks were pretty good this year. We sat out on Billy's roof and watched them. That was kind of cool. You would've loved it, I think. Next year, I'll have my 'Camino. We can get a blanket and put in the back of it, watch the fireworks in style.*

*Okay – like you always say, that's enough of that. I'm ending this letter so I can put it in the mail 'cause I know you won't write me about the grave-yard until you get this reply.*

*Shame on you for keeping me in suspense. You know I have no patience!*

*Your (tall, handsome) Jase*


*P.S. I can't listen to CCR anymore. They remind me too much of Rusty. I have to turn off the radio when they come on. Especially "Fortunate Son." That song says it all. The government took my brother and sent him off to Vietnam. Now he's . . . lost. To quote John Fogerty, he "ain't no fortunate one."*


July 16th

Dearest Jase,

My heart is breaking for you. I love Creedence Clearwater

Revival. But now the words have a different meaning. Every lyric seems steeped in sadness. I can't believe Rusty is still missing in action. I wish I could hug you and make it all better.

Sorry for the cliffhanger trick in my last letter. I couldn't resist. Here's what happened with the graveyard. It was on July 4th and we went to visit Big Steve. He said a friend of his had died and left some things that should have gone to his family, but no one ever came for them. How awful is that? No one even mourned him when he died—except Big Steve, I guess.

Can you believe the guys in prison don't even care about July 4th or any holiday? According to my dad, every day's the same except for Christmas and sometimes that day is even worse if they can't see their kids or some family member. He said he always prayed that I was having a good Christmas with Gran and Gramps. I'll bet it was lonely for him on holidays. I'll bet Aunt Sophia went every year. I could ask her, or him, but do I really want to know? I think I'm beginning to understand that thing Gramps always says about how ignorance is bliss.

I'm also beginning to understand how time leaves things behind. I mean, even though I'm just a kid (according to YOU!), it seems like I've lost a lot of time that I will never get back. It's sad to think about. Even sadder to think Big Steve might not ever get out of this place. That's another one of the things I'm kind of afraid to ask about.

But back to his deceased friend, Jase, the man was a bank robber! My dad said they got acquainted in the license plate shop—they make car license plates, millions of them. You should see the tiny little plates he made for my bike, they have my name on them—one for the front and one for the back.

Anyhow, he said this guy admitted he was young and desperate when he robbed the bank (three banks actually) and that his family never forgave him. Even his wife divorced him and married another man while he was in prison.

Big Steve says he thinks the guy died of a broken heart. That's when I told him that I would never desert him that way,

nor would Aunt Sophia, but I guess he already knew that about her. She's the only other visitor he ever has.

Anyhow, the bank robber was also an artist. Maybe he learned how in prison. He painted pictures of animals and clowns and landscapes that he hoped he could give his children someday. He had two kids, both girls, but they never came to see him after his wife remarried.

Big Steve really seemed to like the guy. Or maybe he just felt sorry for him. He said the unfortunate man had a really strange childhood. He was very poor, and suffered lots of abuse from his parents.

Isn't that the worst thing you ever heard? I know it doesn't excuse anything, but still, it's sad. Big Steve said the guy was on his own by the age of twelve. Raised himself, you know?

I think he told me all this because he is afraid he warped me by leaving Mom and me in the middle of the night and never coming back. Do you think I'm warped, Jase? Don't answer that! Anyway, back to Jonny, the bank robber . . . since no one came and claimed his belongings after he died, the prison gave them to Big Steve. And he gave them to Aunt Sophia and me.

My dad was allowed to keep one painting in his cell—he said it is a picture of a pheasant in flight.

Did your eyes just pop out of your head like a cartoon?

Mine almost did when Big Steve told me that. He said he thought the bird represented freedom somehow. He said Jonny Jensen copied it off the cover of an old *Field & Stream* magazine. So the point of this whole story is that Aunt Sophia and I are now in possession of five amazing oil paintings but the one we don't have is the pheasant—the bird that crashed into the picture window that day.

It has to be a clue, I know, but let me tell you the rest of the story.

Like I said, there are five other paintings which the prison allowed Big Steve to give to Aunt Sophia and me. One is a horse pulling an old-fashioned sleigh through the snow, one is a beautiful German shepherd—made me think of your ghost-dog, Lady —one is a sad lavender-suited clown wearing a dark purple derby, and the other two are landscapes, one spring and one winter.

Aunt Sophia told me to take my choice of the paintings. The man was very talented in my opinion. I can't wait for you to see them. I really like the horse pulling the sleigh. It looks like a Christmas card.

But I don't know how I'm going to get them home. I may have to mail them.

Wow, this letter is going on and on, isn't it? Maybe I'll write you a novel. If I keep going I will have to put two stamps on it. Can you believe they jumped up to eight cents? Aunt Sophia says before long it will cost a dime just to mail in her telephone bill.

Back to my "novel-in-progress."

I'm lying here on my little bed with my paper propped on my knee on top of *Dandelion Wine*. I have a desk in the corner, and if I don't finish soon, I may have to move over there under the lamp.

You would love this room. It is so spare and clean. There are windows on two walls and the curtains are navy with yellow, blue, and purple flowers (sort of psychedelic-floral). The bedspread is solid blue with pretty yellow piping around the edge. You know what piping is, right?

I have two big fluffy pillows, too. Aunt Sophia said she

bought them new, just for me. It made me feel really special.

But back to the graveyard. It's called Forever Field. Isn't that fitting? It's a pauper's field or better yet, a potter's field. I looked it up in the dictionary. It means the people buried there, all men from the prison in this case, had no one to claim them or bury them so they're put out there together with no frills just pine boxes and plain cement headstones. Lots of the graves go back to the late eighteen hundreds when the prison was first built.

When I asked how come so many men had no families to look after them, Big Steve said sometimes the men had been incarcerated so long they had no family left, but other times their family members had deserted them like with Jonny-the-bank-robber.

He went on to say that some of the men buried in Forever Field were such bad guys that they had destroyed all ties to their families and rightly so. I think he was talking about murderers and such, but I didn't ask. None of those men are in Big Steve's part of the prison—thank goodness.

Anyhow, on July 4th he told us his friend, Jonny, had been buried in the cemetery for almost a year and no one had ever claimed his paintings or other belongings. Big Steve said he always felt bad about that. Said it was like a black pall hanging over the pheasant painting (which of course reminded me of the black stuff I thought of as Despair).

Big Steve said he was so thrilled we were going to give the paintings a home he wanted us to go out to the cemetery and tell him. Jonny, I mean. He wanted us to go out to the man's grave and tell him I was there, and that I—and Aunt Sophia—are going to give his paintings a good home.

For a minute I thought he was going to ask me to track down Jonny Jensen's daughters and give *them* the paintings, but no. He just asked me to go out to the cemetery and talk to the man's headstone. (I guess I shouldn't have told him about Lady and Mr. Gilpin, the Phantom Pilot.)

I think Big Steve is worried he will wind up in Forever Field, too. But he isn't going to be locked up the rest of his life. I don't think so, anyway. I still haven't asked, but I will get up my nerve before I leave. Anyhow, I would never let him be buried out there. Aunt Sophia wouldn't either, although, now that I've been to Forever Field, it isn't really that bad. It has lots of trees and a nice wrought iron fence.

Aunt Sophia says they could take better care of it, there were some weeds and burrs and stuff, but I think it could have been worse. Though I'd much rather have Big Steve down in Crossroads Cemetery with Mama and Gran. If it comes to that, I mean.

Ugh. I can't believe I'm talking about burying him and I've barely just met him. Why do I keep getting sidetracked? I'm trying to tell you I went to Forever Field and there I met another phantom. The Phantom of Forever. Can you believe it? I needed *you* there.

I know you're probably saying, "What happened, Stevie, what happened?" So okay, here's what happened (yes, I thought about saving it for another letter just to be mean, but even I'm not that ornery), there we were, Aunt Sophia and me. Uncle Burney hardly ever comes. I get the feeling he doesn't do much where Big Steve is concerned. Aunt Sophia doesn't say anything when I ask her if Uncle Burney will drive us, but her mouth sort of goes thin and turns down on one side. It makes me think they may have had an argument about her spending every Sunday at the prison.

Anyway, it was July 4th. We'd been to the prison already, and that's always good and bad. It makes me feel good to see him and hug him and to know I have a dad when I thought all those years that I didn't, but it also makes me really sad when I have to leave there without him. But this day we weren't going right back to Aunt Sophia's.

The day was so pretty. Very, very, hot, but so wide and so still and so quiet, as if the place was just waiting. Waiting on me, perhaps. And this is a pauper's field remember, so there aren't any fancy headstones or anything. There were a few little flags stuck on some of the graves, but not many.

Have you seen pictures of Arlington Cemetery, all those white crosses? That's sort of how this is, only they aren't crosses, they're just small, old-fashioned headstones all the same shade of gray except for the ones that have moss (or is it mold?) growing on them. Also, they aren't lined up. They're kind of haphazard. Some are tilting and some are taller or shorter than the others because the ground has sunk in, and even the graves are not very regular. It isn't an ugly place, but it all has kind of a forgotten air. You know what I mean?

We went straight over from the prison—it's outside the grounds—and there we were, wandering around, looking for Jonny Jensen in this sea of gray headstones, and I suddenly got that strange deaf feeling where your ears stop hearing and everything seems to stand perfectly still. You know that feeling? Aunt Sophia was walking up and down the messy rows, very methodically, reading each and every name, and I was just standing there, looking at something in the distance, waiting for my hearing to come back, and my senses to reappear. And then I saw it, the black shape. That amorphous *something*. It was floating just off the ground, surrounding one of the graves.

As I watched, it began to dissipate and there she stood, a female figure bending over one of the headstones. She appeared to be wearing a short red coat.

Still deaf, as if I'd stuffed my head with cotton, I took off toward the woman as fast as I could without running. Aunt Sophia didn't even look up. About halfway there, my hearing began to come back and I caught the sound of fluttering wings overhead.

But there was no large bird nearby, just the snippet of song from a mockingbird and the buzz of a locust, that sweet sound that says summer like nothing else. Way off in the distance I could barely make out the deep bass note of an eighteen-wheeler on the highway.

Without acknowledging me, the woman turned away and took off across the scrubby grass. I wanted to call out, but I didn't think it was appropriate to yell in a cemetery.

I kept my eye on the stone she'd been visiting, so I wouldn't mix it up with all the others, and when I got even with it, I raised my eyes to look for her. She was nowhere to be seen, but —you're not going to believe this—I could see her footprints as she walked away. They were just see-through shapes on top of the wild grass. They barely bent the blades and then they were gone. Jase, it reminded me of those Arthur Murray dance steps you can order from TV Guide. You know the ones you stick on the floor to help you learn to cha-cha, or waltz?

I don't know who the woman is. Grief is private, I guess. Especially in a cemetery like this. Some people might not want to be seen visiting these graves. There are probably some really bad men buried here.

When I could no longer see her or her footprints, I glanced down at the stone and was not at all surprised to see that the name engraved on it was Jonny Jensen, Jr.

Kneeling down to get a better look, I felt a chill breeze slip over my skin. There on the curved top of the stone was the delicate imprint of a hand. It resembled the image of a handprint on a steamy shower door, only this one was dark, like a shadow, and it appeared to be fading fast.

As I watched, it disappeared almost completely.

I reached out to touch it, thinking her hand must have been wet—you know how concrete darkens when it's wet or damp—but the stone was cold and dry. Triple digit summer day and the headstone felt as cold as ice.

Aunt Sophia came over then. She stood beside me in front of the gravestone. Said she couldn't believe I'd found it. I didn't tell her about the woman, and if she saw the fading handprint, she didn't mention it.

Kneeling on the patchy green grass near the base of the stone, I whispered the message Big Steve had told me. Then I looked up at Aunt Sophia. I didn't know if that was good enough, but she patted my shoulder and smiled. Then we found a handful of pebbles and lined them up on top of the tombstone so we could find it quickly if we visited again.

We walked back to the car together.

As we left, I couldn't resist looking over my shoulder. I thought I saw a shadow beneath the live oaks, but it was impossible to be sure. The chill bumps on the backs of my arms were real enough, though. But the sound of wings again? Of that, I can't be sure.

So, what do you think? Phantom or real live lady-in-red? I'm not going to mention it to my dad, but I will try and visit the grave again the next time I go.

Yawn!

Gotta get ready for bed. Write me soon,

Stevie-girl, ghost chaser

P.S. I went out and found the NS last night and whispered goodnight to you. I've almost worn out the little note you pressed into my palm when I got on the Amarillo-bound bus that day in Crossroads. Just wanted you to know that.

. . .

I signed off on my letter and put it in an envelope. Jase and I were pretty honest with each other, but since I'd been gone from our little hometown, I'd begun to think of him not just as my best-guy-friend and someday-boyfriend, but as my actual boyfriend. After all, we'd shared our first kiss on the camping trip to Crybaby Bridge and we were still together—even though I was here for the moment—so that proved it wasn't just a puppy-love sort of thing. We'd also weathered Hurricane Karla, so to speak, but I sure didn't want to relive those awful moments.

As always, I wanted him to know how much I missed him, and as usual, it was much easier to say in writing than in person.

*July 20th*

*Dear Stevie-girl,*

*I loved your "novel." Keep 'em coming! And don't let my blues get you down. CCR is the best. You enjoy their music for both of us, okay? When Rusty comes home, it will all be different. Everything will be good again.*

*Anyhow, I'm glad you liked my "farewell" note. I meant it, you and me; don't ever forget that. I don't know about Fate, but you and me, we are meant. That's all. Meant to be.*

*But wow. Come on. Finding phantoms by yourself? Or was the lady-in-red a real person? Nah.*

*Those footprints sound too weird to belong to a real person. And the hand print, too. That black-*

ness still scares me though. I don't mind telling you.

No matter where you go, you find a spirit in need. Or rather, they find you. Wonder what this one wants? Do you think she will contact you? Gosh, be careful. I think I should be there with you. Remember the spirit in the Taylor house? It was pretty dangerous, pushed me all the way down the stairs. And your mom's friend at the old elementary school . . . she wasn't dangerous but the situations sure were. Then the ones at Crybaby Bridge almost did you in—that bear—the flood. Okay, I've convinced myself. I need to come up there, or you need to come home.

Face it, Big Steve isn't going anywhere. You can go back and visit him whenever you want, but please, just make plans to come on home. And stay out of that graveyard. Okay? I have a bad feeling about it.

By the way, your Gramps is doing great. He's getting out and everything. I saw him walking around the neighborhood just yesterday when I went to mow Mr. Pearcy's lawn.

I hope you don't mind, but I went ahead and mowed your yard, too. Your gramps said the doc told him he needed to walk around the block every day, but I didn't think he should be pushing the mower—not yet. Mr. Pearcy agreed with me.

The summer is going by fast, but it's dragging, too. Have you read any more good books? I haven't had as much time to read, but I'm learning a lot *about motors. If I don't make it in college, at least I'll have a career as a grease monkey to fall back on.*

*By the way, Skinny keeps all his back issues of Popular Mechanics and Field & Stream under the counter. I didn't even know he liked to hunt and fish but Stevie-girl, you aren't going to believe this. One of the old issues of Field & Stream has a pheasant on the cover. It's flying over a stream.*

*I wonder if it could possibly be the same one your dad's friend looked at while he was doing the pheasant painting. If Skinny doesn't want it anymore, I'll get the cover and mail it to you. It feels like a connection, doesn't it?*

*Skinny might want to keep it, though. It's pretty old. The date on it was from 1927 or '28. They might even be valuable, I don't know. But of course I think it's all pointing toward something. I'm really surprised to think I'm included, way down here in Crossroads, but I don't see how it could possibly be a coincidence. No way.*

*Anyhow, I'm going to go and put this in an envelope so I can mail it on the way to work. I can't believe I LIKE saying that!*

*Take care of yourself, ghost chaser,*
*Your Jase*

I couldn't believe it when I read Jase's letter. A pheasant in flight. That must mean my connection to Jase is even stronger than I thought because obviously he was now involved in the mystery as well. On one hand, I really was surprised, but on the other hand, it made perfect sense. The spirit in the old Taylor mansion is basically what brought us together (her connection to the Phantom Pilot) so perhaps that meant we would always be connected.

Wow. It was almost too much for my tiny mind to comprehend.

I started to write him back immediately, but I got a call from Gramps that upset me and made me feel like an idiot all at the same time.

After a few days, I finally wrote Jase back.


July 26th

Dear Jase,

I'm sorry I didn't write back immediately. I'm so upset I don't know what to do. Gramps called me on the phone. He said I sounded homesick in my last letter and I guess it's still true, although I thought I'd gotten a handle on it. Everything is just so different here.

But that's not why I'm upset.

He said the Widow Conner is a really good cook and they eat dinner together every night.

What does that mean, Jase? I don't really know that woman very well, but I know she colors her hair a horrid shade of red. Way worse than when I was Cherry Valance for Halloween. What is my Gramps thinking? I do need to come home, don't I? Tell me the truth, is she moving into my home while I'm not there?

I'm sorry I'm cranky. I want to come on home, but the trouble is, we didn't get to go visit Big Steve this past Sunday because Uncle Burney's car broke down and he had to take Aunt Sophia's car when he got called in to work. The next time we can visit is August first. After that, I'm going to tell them I'm ready to buy my ticket home.

I wish I'd brought Sarey with me. I could use a good hug right now, even if it would only be from my old doll. That's sounds stupid, doesn't it? You're right, I'm nothing but a little kid and I don't want that woman moving into my house and trying to take my Gran's place at the kitchen sink. She would probably move the radio. She would probably change everything.

Am I being selfish? I know my Gramps gets lonely, and he changed his whole life when he took in Mom and me all those years ago. I am selfish. Just a selfish little kid.

I'm sorry. Now you see why I haven't written. The letters I tore up were even worse than this one. I might not mail this one, either.

Just me,

Stevie-girl

P.S. I hope you are still enjoying your job.

I stuffed it in an envelope, stuck the stamp on it, and walked it down to the mailbox before I could chicken out. I knew Jase would be worried because he hadn't heard from me. I just didn't know how to fake being happy. Maybe that was a learned skill.

July 27th

Dear Jase,

Ignore that whiny letter I mailed yesterday. I was just having a moment of self-pity. I'm not only a little kid; sometimes I'm a big ol' baby. A crybaby.

Right now, I'm lying here on my almost-psychedelic bedspread looking at the paintings we brought home.

The horse pulling the sleigh is still my favorite. It reminds me of *The Black Stallion* or maybe *Black Beauty*.

Aunt Sophia hung the winter and spring paintings in her den, but she wasn't as big a fan of the purple clown. She hung it in the hallway. I pass it each time I leave my room. There is something about that painting that I can't quite put my finger on. . . but don't worry. I'm sure it's nothing. I just really wanted to tell you to IGNORE that last stupid letter I sent. I'm back to my old self now.

Just me,
Stevie-girl

P.S. Did I tell you there's also a German shepherd painting that really reminds me of Lady? I've got it in my room to remind me of you.

There. That should do it. That's how you fake happy, or at least un-worried.

I put a stamp on the letter and put it in the mailbox. For the first time I wondered if there was a faster way to mail a letter. I'd heard of first class, but I didn't really know what it meant.

I mentally shrugged my shoulders and turned to go back to the house. What's done is done.

*August 2nd*
*Dear Stevie,*
*Don't worry about your Gramps and the widow. I don't think anything serious is going to happen. Your Gramps is just lonely right now, like you said. Maybe they are good friends like you and*

me. Not that we are ONLY friends, I didn't mean that—you know you are my BEST friend in the whole world, and more—but they could be only friends, right? Jeez, that wasn't very helpful, was it? For a wanna-be author I sure don't write letters very well.

Hey, ghost chaser, I tried to call you the other day, after I got your last letter, but I guess y'all were gone somewhere, there was no answer. Then I tried again the next day and it said out of order. Is everything all right? I know I've got the correct number. Let me know, soon. Please.

I guess I could go ask your Gramps—I just don't want to worry him, you know?

How did the visit go with Big Steve? I keep thinking I will get a letter saying you are on your way home now, but I know it's too soon if you just saw him yesterday.

You know I was just teasing about you being a KID. Stop saying that now, you hear?

And by the way, you're entitled to feel jealous of the Widow Conner—that's your home she's encroaching upon. (How about that word—encroaching—quite writerly don't ya think?)

Anyhow, stop scolding yourself. You've had so many losses, who could blame you for wanting things to stay the same for a while? I know I sure don't.

And now for the music and war news:

Unfortunately no news on Rusty. I hope no news

*really is good news. At least we haven't had news of his death or capture. That's something, right?*

*As for music, I found a new song for you, Stevie-girl. "Never Can Say Goodbye." It's by The Jackson 5. I thought you'd really like this one—and not just because it's about saying goodbye but because it's just such a good tune.*

*Our radio station is playing The Temptations all the time. "Just my Imagination," is a great song, too.*

*I can't wait until you get home so we can go to the music store and flip through the new records together. I still go every Saturday when they get the new 45s in, but it's not the same. Every song reminds me of you.*

*Take care of yourself, and write me soon. And hey, did you see that moon last night, and the North Star? I hoped you were looking up at the same time I was . . .*

*Your Jase*

*P.S. Skinny gave me the old Field & Stream magazine and I took it home thinking I might mail you the cover like I said, but when I went to tear it off, I noticed the address label. Stevie, this magazine was originally sent to someone in Someplace, Arizona. I couldn't read the person's name or the city, it was rubbed away, but anyhow at least it's a state. Probably nothing, but then again, who knows? Maybe you could ask Big Steve . . . I'm going to keep the magazine here (and leave the cover on it) because it seems important. I don't want to risk mailing it unless you want me to.*

Once again, I couldn't believe it when I got Jase's letter. He'd tried to call me, and I'd missed it. Then the next day he'd gotten an out of order message.

But the phone is working fine. Or at least it has been as far as I know. I'm really depressed now. Maybe I should go ahead and ask Aunt Sophia to get me that return ticket. I can't just leave in the middle of a mystery though. I have to find out about the woman in the red jacket. First, however, I've got to make Jase a birthday card. I don't feel right asking Aunt Sophia to take me to buy one. Her and Uncle Burney are having enough trouble getting around with just the one car.

Folding my unlined paper in half, I drew a fat bottle of maple syrup on the front, shaded it in with the colored pencils I'd brought from home, and then I wrote a silly poem inside.

Roses are red
Violets are purple
You're as sweet
As maple surple

It was an old rhyme and a silly one, but I loved it. My Gramps always said it to me when I was small. That made me really miss him so as soon as I finished the card and put it in the envelope, I sat down to write Gramps, too.

But before I even started the letter, the phone rang.

I just knew it would be Jase, but it was my Gramps instead.

I nearly burst into tears at the sound of his voice. Later, I went ahead and wrote him anyway.

Thursday, August 5th

Dear Gramps,

It was so good to hear your voice. I'm sorry I made you worry—I didn't mean to do that. I am a little homesick, you were right. When everyone is at work and it's just me here with the radio and TV, I go a little stir crazy. I've already read all the interesting books in the house, so I have to make another trip to the library. I may try that tomorrow if Aunt Sophia says it's okay. The library and the music store, those are my goals. And getting to visit Big Steve one more time, of course.

Uncle Burney said the garage had to order some part for his car, that's why it's taking so long to fix. He was really steamed about it so I don't know if we'll be able to go next Sunday or not. I guess it depends on whether he has to work. If he doesn't need the car, Aunt Sophia can take us. He never goes with us.

I hope you are still feeling well and not trying to do too much. I'm glad Jase mowed the grass so you don't have to worry about that. And I'm thankful the Widow Conner is feeding you so well.

I don't have any other news . . . like I said, not much goes on here when everyone is at work.

Take care of yourself and I hope I will see you soon.

All my love,

Stevie-girl

I didn't hesitate to get Gramps's letter in the mail. I wanted him to get it as soon as possible. My heart was sick I missed my

Gramps so much. Now I understood the term heartsick. I did not like it.

August 6th

Dear Jase, Happy Birthday!

I don't know what happened – I just got back the letter I sent to you with your card. It looks like I didn't put a stamp on it, but I know I did.

It makes me wonder if I'm getting all of your letters. I mean if you aren't getting mine then it stands to reason . . .

Well, anyhow, I'm sending you another to let you know I'm fine and I really was thinking of you on your birthday. In fact, I'll just stick that letter in with this one (along with your card – again.)

In other news, the purple clown painting looks odd. I can't quite place it, but it looks different somehow. If I didn't know better, I'd swear it's changing colors.

It appears that the clown's dark purple hat is now lilac and his lavender suit has gone almost white. Do you think it's because they've been in storage all this time and now . . . I don't know, the light is somehow ruining the paint?

I haven't been back to see Big Steve yet. Uncle Burney's car is still in the shop. Maybe he won't have to work this Sunday and we can take Aunt Sophia's car but he gets a lot of overtime in his job with the highway department so who knows if he'll be off.

If nothing else, maybe Aunt Sophia and I can take the bus. They don't let kids my age (yes, I said kids) go to the prison alone so I have to wait for her to say yes or no.

I don't know what's wrong with the phone. Gramps called just a couple of days ago. But after I read your letter, I picked up the receiver to check it and it still seems to be working fine.

Yes, please hold on to that *Field & Stream* magazine. I want to see it when I get home. It does feel like a connection. A deep connection. (Not surprising is it?)

By the way, I did it. I turned into Stevie-the-Brave today. I actually found my way to the music store after the library. I got the 45s of "Just My Imagination," and "Never Can Say Good-bye." I'd heard them both on the radio, but you're right. They've become my *new* favorites. Of course, I still love Janis. I wish I'd brought my records with me, but I couldn't do that on the bus. And it would be too wasteful to buy the same records over again, wouldn't it? Besides, Amarillo has a really cool radio station that plays the best music all the time. YOU WOULD LOVE IT.

My trip downtown wasn't bad at all. It was a straight shot. Can you believe they charge a dollar for a library card? I got my own card since I didn't have Aunt Sophia with me. Now I have two library cards—wouldn't it be cool to get a card from every town you ever visit?

Anyhow, I checked out a book called *Red Sky at Morning* by Richard Bradford. I've only read a few chapters, but I adore this book. I also checked out *The Black Stallion Returns*. You know how I wore out the first one. I hope the second one is as good, though I don't see how it could be.

After the library, which is GREAT, just like our little library back home (but bigger), I felt so *brave* I asked the next bus driver where I should go to get a cheeseburger. He took me to a stop near The Canton Café. Can you believe it, me, in a café alone, having lunch? Well, I wasn't really alone. I had my books. (You have to read *Red Sky at Morning*. You *have* to.)

Then I caught another bus (I still miss my bike, and you, but I'm getting this bus thing down pretty good, don't you think?) and that's when I went to the Go Low Records store (a strange name for a cool place) where a guy with long wavy hair and a denim vest (with a peace sign on the back) showed me to a huge bin where the 45s were located.

I flipped through them for quite a while, wishing you were there. The guy kept coming over to check on me, so I told him the record I wanted and he knew right where to find it.

When I went to check out, I couldn't help glancing at my watch as he rang me up. He said, "Are you in a hurry?" I told him the bus driver said I should keep an eye on the time even though I knew it made me sound like that kid you think I am, but he didn't laugh or anything. He was really nice. He even teased me about my braid by saying he bet my hair would be as wavy as his if I didn't wear it in a pigtail. Then he tweaked the end of it just like you always do.

Anyhow, I think you are going to LOVE the record I got you for your birthday. I won't tell you which one it is. You'll just have to wait.

Can you believe they have listening booths in that store? I didn't try them, though. I wasn't that brave. There were a couple of people in separate booths with headphones on. I couldn't believe it. I wanted to know what they were listening to. One man, an older guy who had white hair and a shiny black suit, was tipped back in a chair with the headphones on and I'd swear he was asleep. He never opened his eyes the whole time I was there.

I didn't get to stay long. Brave or not, I heeded the bus driver's warning not to miss the bus when it came back because the one after that would be the last one of the day, and it was usually full. I never even thought of a bus filling up, did you?

Jase, I wish you could see downtown Amarillo. It's a lot bigger than Crossroads, but it isn't scary. There are some tall buildings that are ten or fifteen stories high. I want to go inside and ride an elevator—but I think I might need you for that. I don't know if I'll ever be that brave alone. But if I stay much longer I am going to try and catch a matinee at The Paramount Theater. I will take a picture of it for you. I know you would like the marquee. Right now it's showing John Wayne in *Big Jake*. I could actually smell the popcorn when I walked by. And the music store clerk said the Saturday matinee only costs fifty cents. He said the theater has the most beautiful sunburst painting on the ceiling. I can't wait to see what that looks like. Maybe I can do that tomorrow or the next day. I'm tired of sitting at home doing nothing.

The bus driver said if I like the way downtown looks now, I should see it at Christmas time. He said the town and the merchants go all out, stringing lights across the street and playing Christmas carols on every corner—kind of like Crossroads, only on a grander scale.

Anyhow, I've been up and down Polk Street so many times now that I think I could find my way around pretty easily. Polk is where all the shops are. The guy at the music store told me that some astronomers determined (somehow) that the street sign at the corner of 6th and Polk is actually the very center of the ENTIRE UNIVERSE. Can you believe that—or do you think he was pulling my leg? He also said if I came downtown on a weekend night I would see all the kids "dragging Polk." I told him the kids in Crossroads did that, too, dragged Main— and the courthouse square—but to hear him tell it, there would be hundreds of cars out, not just a couple dozen. He said on Saturday night kids come from all the little towns around, too.

I can't believe how much I like this place. I always thought I would hate a big town. Oh, one more reason you would like Amarillo . . . it's on Route 66. The highway runs right through town. Isn't that the road Jack Kerouac followed? Are you still going to do that someday, explore the country, writing poetry and fiction with a dog (or possibly your best friend) by your side?

We could get library cards in every town. I don't know how we'd earn any money though do you, Grease Monkey?

Well, enough of all that. I'm going to stop for now and put this letter (and card) in the mail. I'm putting two stamps on the envelope this very instant—I swear I am—so you should have it (and your card) in three days. Take care and don't work too hard.

Just me,

Stevie-girl

P.S. I can't wait to hear all about your birthday.

I put the thick envelope in the mailbox and raised the flag again. Then I went inside and watched a soap opera on TV.

When the mailman came down the block, whistling as always, I watched to make sure he took my letter to Jase. There was no reason for it to come back this time. I had a feeling things were beginning to get squirrelly.

First the black shape near the prison turnoff, then the pheasant, then the lady-in-the-red-jacket, and then the paintings going pale. Now Jase is having trouble getting my mail and he's having trouble calling me.

I'm beginning to think I need to make a plan. To do something instead of waiting for the next thing to happen. But what can I do? I can't tell Aunt Sophia. I told Big Steve about The Phantom Pilot and the old Taylor house, and that's when things started going haywire.

Now I can't even get back to the prison to visit him.

Why is this so hard? If a spirit needs my help, all it has to do is ask. I can't think of any reason I should be prevented from helping.

What's the problem here?

I got out *Red Sky at Morning* and tried to read. In spite of all that had happened, I was soon lost in the fictional past, growing up and falling in love with a couple of kids in New Mexico in the 1940s.

*August 9th*

*Dear Stevie,*

*I LOVE THE CARD!*

*I tried to call you again and it just rang and rang and rang. You were probably at the music store visiting your new friend.*

*You didn't miss much on my birthday. It was okay. It wasn't a big celebration. Mom made a red velvet cake, my favorite, and Dad made homemade ice cream to go with it. It was delicious.*

*Billy Bob and Derol both came over and ate cake and ice cream, and then we all TOOK A RIDE IN MY NEW EL CAMINO!!!*

*I finally got it, Stevie. It was the best birthday present ever, and I gave it to myself. Actually it would have been the best ever if you'd been riding with me, but you will, soon. I promise.*

*I passed both the written test and the driving test on the first try, nothing to it. I've got my paper hardship license, but the real one won't be in for four weeks. I can't believe it, can you?*

*Anyhow, what about the painting, is it still changing colors? That's downright weird. Not surprising, but weird.*

*Have you been back to Forever Field yet? I know you probably want to go alone, since I'm not there, but since you can't go to the prison alone, I guess you can't go to the prison graveyard alone either, right?*

*What ever you do, please, be careful. The woman-in-the-red-jacket is probably a phantom, and there could be others nearby.*

*Now. Tell me more about your trip downtown to the music store. Have you gone again? It sounds like the clerk was really flirting with you. Tell him to keep his hands off those pigtails! And even though I know you'd like to go to a movie, if he invites you then you just tell him . . . tell him . . . well. Tell him you already have a boyfriend.*

*Can't wait to see you,*

*Your Jase*

*P.S. I couldn't see the NS last night. Too cloudy. But I caught glimpses of the moon. I hope you did, too. Buddy and I were both thinking of you—I took him for a midnight ride. Come home, soon, ghost-hunter.*

I lay back in Uncle Burney's recliner with Jase's letter clutched to my chest. Boyfriend. I have a boyfriend. Of course I'd thought of him that way (to myself), but we'd never spoken of it. Except for the note he'd pressed into my palm when I got on the bus back in Crossroads, that is. But still, for him to say it, to come right out and write it in a letter, that was something. That was special.

I guess I'd avoided even thinking of that subject after the fiasco with Karla at Crybaby Bridge. I'd felt so stupid when I got jealous of her, my ex-best-friend, that now that the shoe was on the other foot, I welcomed a bit of redemption. Not very nice of me, I know. But no one ever accused me of being perfect. That's for sure.

August 13th
     Dear Jase,

Are you *jealous*? I would never try to make you jealous. That's the funniest thing I've ever heard. Remember how upset I got when Karla kept flirting with you on our camping trip? I ran off and got in trouble. Don't you do anything like that, okay? I promise you the music store guy was just being nice. He looked like kind of a hippie. Besides, no one can hold a candle to you and you know it (don't let that go to your big ol' writer's head). But you must know how much I miss you and all the folks (and Buddy) back home.

     I guess that's why it was so nice to encounter a friendly face. Between Aunt Sophia's house and the prison, I haven't seen a lot of kids my age (there's that darn K word again).
     Anyhow, the painting . . .
     It's almost gone, Jase. I mean the colors are almost gone. Now it looks like a whiteout snowstorm. The kind I remember reading about in the *Little House on the Prairie* books. If I look closely, it seems I can see snow flying—sideways—across the canvas.
     Aunt Sophia thinks the paint was somehow defective. Should I tell her about the horse and sleigh in my winter landscape painting? It hangs in my room so maybe she doesn't notice it as much . . .
     The horse is turning his head, Jase. He used to be looking

forward, now he (I call it a he because it looks just like The Black Stallion) appears to be glancing over his right shoulder. Glancing over his right shoulder at me, lying on my bed. Looking right out of the picture at me. But that isn't all, as the Cat in the Hat said, "Oh, no! That's not all."

The driver of the sleigh is no longer a man in a top hat. Now it's a little clown in a purple derby.

Yep. You read that right. The pictures are getting all mixed up, as if to get my attention, to show me something, but I don't know what. It's a little freaky. But not nearly as freaky as flying garden tools and cutout newspaper letters the way The Phantom Pilot communicated with us. Remember? Our first taste of phantom hunting was trying to figure out his message. And we did.

Now I'll have to figure this one out, too. And soon. Before I leave. That's why I've got to revisit Forever Field. We go tomorrow. Wish me luck. I think the spirit of the artist is trying to say something to me in those paintings. What else could be causing the odd changes? It's as if something is sending the little purple clown somewhere in a snowstorm. And the horse is looking at me to make sure I follow? I don't know. Is that a stretch?

On the other hand, with all the phone and mail problems we've been having, I also feel as if something is trying to keep me from communicating with you. Why do you suppose that would be?

Anyhow. Yes, I look at the NS every night. And the moon, too. Now I will imagine both you *and* Buddy when I go out to look. Aunt Sophia's house has a lovely yard with a big porch swing. It's really nice to sit out there at night and write to you while I watch the moon.

And you can think of me in that setting (I thought you'd like that term, wordsmith) the way I picture you and Buddy out in your back field. I like that image. I don't know which picture my imagination likes better, you riding Buddy across the field at midnight, or you driving the El Camino while tanning your left arm. Haha. I can't wait to get home and go for a ride.

Just me,

Stevie

P.S. Why do you think the painting of the German shepherd doesn't change? It always looks the same. It's just the clown, and the horse pulling the sleigh that keeps changing. I haven't seen any changes in Aunt Sophia's Spring and Winter scenes either.

If you have a theory, I'd love to hear it.

*August 16th*

*Stevie, Stevie, Stevie,*

*Of course a phantom is trying to contact you. Aren't you scared? I mean with the paintings changing almost right before your eyes? No. I guess you wouldn't be. If anything did appear, you'd just whack it with a bread sack, right?*

*Just a very short note today. I'm getting a little concerned that I can't call you on the phone. I even had the operator check the number. She said it was the right number, and so I had her to dial it for me and she said it was in good working order, but no one appeared to be home.*

*What the heck?*

*I'm pretty sure you were home at eight o'clock this morning. That's when I called. That's the third time this has happened. I've tried to call in the morning, in the afternoon, and in the evening when I thought you would all be there, but it's the same thing every time. It just rings and rings and rings.*

*Can you call me? I'm getting worried. Especially since your letters don't always seem to make it here. I loved the birthday card, by the way, did I tell you that already? Call me collect. I've okayed it with Mom and Dad. Call me anytime before 3:45 p.m. that's when I leave to go to work.*

*Your "Sweet" Jase*

August 19th

Dear Jase,

I don't know what is going on with the phones. After I got your letter, I immediately tried to call you collect like you said. It was about 2:30 p.m. but there was no answer.

I'll just tell you my news now in case I don't get to talk to you anytime soon. The car part finally came in so we went to visit Big Steve.

Before we went I checked the paintings—the used-to-be-purple-clown picture is no longer just a whiteout painting.

Now it has a huge black hole in the center of it. Not a real hole in the canvas, no. A painted on hole. Like where a spaceship crashed or something. I'm not kidding. It's the strangest thing. I'm going to see if Aunt Sophia will let me take a picture of it with her camera. She said there were only a couple more exposures on the roll and then she would get it developed.

Jase, I know you would recognize this. The place looks like a picture I've seen somewhere—probably in an encyclopedia or something—but I just can't place it. Or hey, maybe it's something I read, like in a science fiction story by Ray Bradbury or George Orwell.

When I showed it to my aunt she just shuddered and gripped her elbows with her hands. She said, "I'm glad Burney doesn't come down here toward your room. Don't tell him about this. He won't like it. Not at all." She hurried on down the hall, but I stopped her before she made it back to the living room.

"But what do you think is wrong with the painting?" I asked.

She shrugged, but she wouldn't look at it again. "It looks like it's self-destructing," she said. "Maybe we should get rid of them. All of them." She closed her eyes. "I know they wouldn't let us take them back to Steve, you can never take anything in, but I just don't know what else to do with them." Then she glanced out the window into the back yard where the barbecue grill is located.

Jase, I think she means to burn them. I don't really blame her—it's very strange the way they keep changing—but I'm afraid if she tries to destroy them, something terrible might happen.

After that, I didn't dare tell her about my sleigh-ride scene and how the horse is now looking at me, and the driver has changed to a clown.

I still feel like the painting is saying, "follow me." But follow them where? And why is the clown gone from one picture only to appear in another, in a snowstorm at that? Snow seems to be a clue. Snow, and traveling somewhere. Maybe the clown represents the artist. He seems so sad and desperate.

I didn't tell Big Steve any of this yet. In the end, it was just too strange. Besides, he had news of his own for a change. He says a lawyer thinks he might be able to get out on parole. The lawyer says he seems to have "fallen through the cracks" and no one should have spent this much time in prison on a DWI. Not even a third one with an assault charge.

I'll keep you posted on that.

After we left my dad, I asked Aunt Sophia if we could visit Forever Field, but she said no, Uncle Burney wanted us to come straight home. I like my uncle, a lot. He works hard, he barbecues great hamburgers, and he even jokes around sometimes. But where my dad is concerned, there is something odd. Could he resent his own wife's brother?

I was disappointed we couldn't go out to Forever Field, but there was nothing I could do about it. I'm wondering if I could take the bus there tomorrow, on a weekday. Maybe the rules for visiting the cemetery are different and I can go alone. I'm going to check into it. I'll also check on the bus schedules.

I can't wait to hear from you.

Just me,

Your Stevie


I couldn't wait for a letter from Jase. I had to go ahead and tell him what was going on. Once again, I tried to call him on the phone, but when I picked up the receiver all I got was waaa, waaa, waaa. It reminded me of how the teacher sounds on the Charlie Brown Christmas movie (one of mine and Gramps's holiday traditions back home is watching that show on TV every year while drinking hot chocolate and eating popcorn).


August 21st

Dear Jase,

The summer is going by so fast. I really thought I would be home in time for your birthday, but now I'm beginning to wonder if I'll even be home in time for school. Like the phones nowadays, things don't always work the way they should.

Today, I'm going to visit Forever Field. I'm sitting here waiting on the bus right now. I called the cemetery office yesterday, and they said I do not have to be accompanied by an adult to visit.

The phone worked fine when I called them, Jase, but when I tried to call you collect, I couldn't even get the operator. All I heard was waaa, waaa, waaa. That makes me almost certain something is preventing us from talking to each other.

Anyhow, I wrote a note to Jonny Jensen about his paintings. (That's why I couldn't go to the cemetery yesterday. I took so much time writing and trying to call that I missed the bus.) Anyway, remember how I told you about the painted hole on the once-purple-clown-picture? Well, now I can definitely see white speckles in the black center. When I look away, from the corner of my eye, the snow starts falling, like in a movie. Now I have no doubt, it is definitely a crash site of some kind.

The snow is falling in the crash site. I hope it doesn't obscure it before I figure out what—or where—it is. After giving it a lot of thought, and making lots of freewriting notes about all that has happened, I've decided the painting might be a clue to where Jonny Jensen's daughters are living. I mean he painted the clown for them, right? Now the clown is driving the horse and sleigh through a snowstorm, which seems to have carried over to the original clown painting, so it *must* have something to do with them. What else would be this important?

You don't think Jonny Jensen is trying to show us where he hid the money from his crimes or something, do you? That does it. I have to go back to the library and try to find some information on those bank robberies. Maybe it isn't about the daughters at all. Maybe it's all about the money . . . but wait. Even if someone was trying to show us to some sort of "buried treasure," who is left to benefit from it?

The daughters? Nah. If there was a hidden treasure, I'm sure I would've heard something about it.

Listen to me. Just guessing. I have to make a trip downtown tomorrow, that's all there is to it. Sure wish you were here to go with me, that would be so much fun, showing you the sights.

One thing I do know, this has to be Jonny Jensen, or his phantom, trying to tell me *something*. That's why I have to go. I have to see the grave again, for myself. I seriously think I'm supposed to reunite the paintings with the girls. It doesn't seem like he is all about money. Anyhow, I'm going to believe it's all about the love between a father and his daughters. That's what I told him in this new note that I plan to leave on his grave.

Okay, enough of all that. Tell me more about your work and about your new car. It will be fun to go for a ride.

I have to stop now. The bus is coming. I can't wait to see Forever Field again, but I also can't wait to get back home (here) and check those paintings. Especially the clown. It seems to change hourly. Sometimes right before my very eyes.

Write me soon . . .

Just me,

Your Stevie-girl

*August 21st*

*Dear Stevie,*

*As usual, something strange is going on. I don't want to alarm you, but it seems that something is trying to keep us apart. My last letter came back to me. Why would that be? Look here, this is what I know so far (and it's freaking me out).*

*The facts:*

1. *I can't call you*
2. *Your letters don't always get to me (now mine aren't always getting to you, either)*
3. *You're not always able to see your Dad . . . but you ARE able to visit the cemetery – wait! I think that's it!*

*Something or someone is determined to keep you there so you can keep going to the cemetery. Maybe to help the phantom lady. The one in the red jacket. Doesn't that make sense? I mean, look . . . things seemed to go haywire right after you got the paintings and went to the cemetery to give Jonny Jensen your dad's message.*

*Oh, and then you told me that after one more visit with Big Steve you'd be ready to come home. That's when the car broke down, the phone started acting weird, and the paintings began to change. Voila! The spirit is going to prevent you from leaving until you figure out the message.*

*The question is, what do we do about it? I'm no use to you at all down here at home.*

*I may show up on your doorstep soon. I just have to okay the time off with Skinny, and get permission from my dad. Which may not be so easy.*

*Don't worry. I'll figure it out. I think you
need me.*
*Your Jase*
*P.S.*
*What do the paintings look like now?*


August 23rd

Dear Jase,

It's been a while since I've heard from you. I'm not sure if you're getting my letters at all. I'll keep writing them, just in case. I tried to call you again, while my aunt and uncle were at work, but just like you said about my phone, yours just rang and rang. At least I didn't get waa, waa, waaa this time.

I don't know what else to do, or how to get in touch with you.

I even tried calling my Gramps, but his just rang and rang, too.

Anyhow, I went to the cemetery. The bus driver didn't seem to want to let me off the bus. At first, I thought uh-oh, the phantom is going to keep me from going in, but no. The driver was just a kind old man worried I shouldn't be going in there alone. I guess not too many kids do this. Well, not by bus at least.

After a minute or so, I convinced him it was all right, I think my winning smile and gregarious (how's that for another writerly word?) nature had something to do with it—ha ha.

Now get this, when I stepped down from the bus, the day was hot and sunny. But as soon as I walked through the iron gates, the temperature dropped and if I turned my head just right, I could see icicles dripping from the tree branches. If I looked straight ahead everything appeared normal. When I turned around to see if the bus had left, the wrought iron fencing was barely visible through the cold mist. The bus was nowhere in sight. I hadn't even heard it pull away.

Jase, it felt like I'd walked into another dimension, one that was almost but not quite there.

I retraced my path from before, slipping on my jacket as I went. Did I tell you I borrowed Aunt Sophia's red jacket? (Good thing she is so petite.) It was a spur of the moment thing. She'd worn it to work one day and it made me think of the phantom lady. So—as my Gramps would say—it seemed like a good idea at the time. I didn't tell her I borrowed it; I just left her a note in case it got stained or something.

Don't roll your eyes like that, Jason Lee, I know what you're thinking. You think I'm courting disaster by dressing like the phantom lady, but don't worry. Nothing happened. Well, not much anyway.

First, I went right to the grave. I didn't see anyone, no one at all. Hardly any people ever come here—that's the sad part. Our rocks were still lined up on top of the grave, but a new one had been added. A small piece of beautiful turquoise sat right in the middle of the head stone.

I knew it was a clue of some sort, so I put it in my pocket—I felt like a thief when I slipped it in there—then all sound went away. I'd gone deaf again. As soon as it was safely hidden in the pocket of my jeans (I didn't even trust it in the pocket of the red jacket; what if there was a hole or I forgot to get it back out?) snowflakes began to fall.

No kidding.

Snowflakes falling through a cold mist in the-dog-days-of-summer-August. I held out my arm and watched them land and melt on the red jacket. Then I leaned down and placed my new note, in an envelope, at the base of the tombstone. I piled some of the rocks on it, and then the snowflakes stopped. They just quit.

The temperature started to rise, crickets began to chirp, and even a mockingbird sang in a live oak nearby.

What a relief.

I took off the red jacket, told Jonny Jensen I was doing my level best to help figure things out, then I turned to leave.

And there she was, the phantom lady, hurrying away, an envelope in her hand.

When I looked down at the grave, my envelope was gone. Jase, I almost passed out. Chills crept up my arms and then my feet fairly launched me away of the grave in pursuit of her, but it was too late. She'd gone invisible again. All I could see was a tinge of red in the distance, where the mist still blurred the fence line, and just as before, I watched in awe as her footprints continued to bend the grass where she had walked.

I know I keep saying this, but I sure wish you were here, Jase. We've seen a lot, you and I, but this is exceedingly weird. It really does remind me of your story about the night you first met Roger Gilpin, The Phantom Pilot.

Why do you think I can't talk directly to the lady-in-the-red-jacket, or any phantom for that matter? Why do they have to be so sneaky, so roundabout? I mean I was standing right there. How could she get the envelope and be halfway across the cemetery before I could take a breath?

Do you think they stop time somehow, or are they just invisible when they're close by? And why are they so darned illusive? Do you think it's because they aren't supposed to be here, or because it would be too traumatic for a live person to actually see them close up? Or are they just trapped somehow, ashamed to be seen because of all their regrets?

I lie awake at night wondering about it. I mean if they can manipulate paintings, leave me objects, cause weather to change in an instant—and appear and disappear at will—why the heck can't they just step up and tell me what they want me to do? It's so frustrating! It's like they are playing a game, but I know they aren't. From our past experience I know how serious it really is for them, and as a result, for me. (And you when you're with me.)

Wait a minute. What did I just say, that they can't be seen up close? But that's not completely true because you did meet Roger Gilpin in person, didn't you? Do you suppose it's because he'd just left his body that very instant? Maybe once they've entered the spirit world, they can't meet us face-to-face anymore. Jeez. It could be anything.

Anyhow . . . long story short, I got on the next bus and went directly to the public library and researched the origin of turquoise. I knew it had to mean something. I figured the lady-in-the-red-jacket left it since she was just there.

In the encyclopedia I found several places where turquoise is mined, most notably New Mexico and Arizona (I didn't bother to look at places outside the United States although it is mined there, too) and then I remembered what you said about the *Field & Stream* cover being mailed to someone in Arizona, so I began looking for a big "crash site" in Arizona.

Look what I found: Winslow, Arizona has a huge meteor crash site called The Barringer Crater. It's where the astronauts trained for the Apollo space missions. (I figured you'd love that!) And it's not too far from the Navajo Indian Reservation where turquoise is mined.

It's coming together, isn't it? I mean, it feels right. Maybe the Jensen daughters (or one of them) live there. Or maybe they used to live there. I wish you'd been there when I read all that, Jase. I got so excited I couldn't even think straight. I knew it was a connection.

After a few minutes of just sitting there, trying to sort it out,

I finally came up with an idea.

I asked the reference librarian for help and she showed me where to get the white pages for Winslow, AZ.

I'm sure you know what I was thinking . . . I immediately looked up the surname, Jensen. Holy cow. There were dozens. I'm sort of stuck now. I don't know how to narrow the list down and I sure can't call them all long distance.

Maybe I'll get another clue.

Now, I'm going to go and put this out in the mailbox and pray that it gets to you.

Just me,

Your Stevie

P.S. No moon last night. Lots of clouds. I couldn't see the dipper at all. But oh, I forgot to tell you, I did look up Jonny Jensen's bank robberies while I was at the library (newspapers on microfiche) and all the money was recovered so that completely blows my lost-treasure theory. Just as well. I liked the father-daughter-connection much better.

————

*August 21st*

*Dear Stevie-girl,*

*Just wondering how you're getting along? Not to pressure you, but are you coming home before school starts? The widow makes a fine cobbler, but she can't scald hot cocoa or bake a pork-chop like you, girl.*

*I'm a little surprised I haven't heard from you lately. I tried to call you and the phone just sounded like a busy signal. I know you're having a big time, but write me a letter—better yet, go ahead and call me collect—I miss you, Stevie-girl. But I'm doing fine, so don't worry.*

*Much love, Gramps*

·  ·  ·

August 23rd

Dear Gramps,

I'm getting a little worried since I haven't heard from you in a while. Is everything okay at home? As I sit here on my bed, writing this, I'm beginning to think maybe I haven't heard from you because of this phone situation. It seems to work fine for Aunt Sophia and Uncle Burney, but I don't get any calls anymore. I even tried to make a collect call to you and then one to Jase but the operator said there was no answer at either place. Even Aunt Sophia remarked on how the phone had stopped ringing. I'm about ready to come home. I miss you so much I'm even ready for school to start back up just so I have an excuse to get on that bus.

That's all for now, Gramps. I love you and I plan on seeing you soon!

Stevie

————

August 24th

Dear Diary,

I'm lying here on my little bed in my home-away-from-home room, sad as sad can be because it seems everyone has deserted me. Oh, I know deep down that probably isn't true, but I'm not getting many letters and no phone calls at all.

I'm just about ready to head home even though I don't know what's going on at Forever Field. I miss my Gramps. And I really miss Jase, too. I've got his birthday gift right here on top of my dresser. It's a new 45rpm of "Crimson and Clover" to replace the one that got broken the first time we went ghost hunting together. I even have a tiny red spot where the record hit my forehead when it flew off the turntable at me. Yeah, I know. It was a long time ago. But the spot still reappears from time to time. I figure it has something to do with my body temperature or . . . spirits. Maybe it's my spirit meter. Haha. (It's good to laugh at yourself, right?)

Anyhow, Diary, since I'm not sure where my letters are going, I will continue to write in this little book (to you) just in case I forget to tell Jase something when I see him. *If I ever do see him again!*

Hey—wait, that's the doorbell. No one ever rings the doorbell in the middle of the day. Not when my aunt and uncle are both at work . . . should I answer it, Diary? Let me look out the window.

Oh my gosh! I dropped the curtain on my bedroom window and streaked to the front door squealing like a banshee. By the time I got the lock open—the darn thing wouldn't turn for some reason —Jase was standing on the porch, laughing his head off.

Launching myself at him seemed like the right thing to do. He caught me easily and I hugged him and kissed him and vowed to never ever let him go. But of course, I had to. He set me back on my feet and looked me up and down. "Did'ja miss me?"

I walloped him and dragged him in the front door. "You know I've been missing you like crazy. How did you get here?" I glanced out at the curb expecting to see his new El Camino, but there was nothing there.

"Naturally, I flew," he said. "You didn't think I'd bring the 'Camino all the way up here, did'ja? It might get dirty." And then he flapped his arms like a big old blond-haired bird. That's when I knew I was dreaming, Diary. That's when my heart began to break.

I woke slowly, not wanting the dream to end, even if it was goofy. Now I'm just sitting here, looking out the window, wishing it were true.

The day is hot; the sun so high the sky looks white instead of blue. If I were home, I might be down at the public pool. Once upon a time, Karla and I spent almost every summer afternoon there. I miss our local radio station, the way the pool manager blared Top 40 all across the water.

The Monkees, The Byrds, Bob Dylan, The Jackson 5, CCR, and Janis Joplin. Always Janis singing "Me & Bobby McGee" or "Get it While You Can." My ex-best friend, Karla, and me. We knew the words to every song . . .

That's all I can write for now, Diary. Tears keep blurring my vision, splotching my ink. I miss my home. Maybe I'll be better tomorrow. Hey—maybe it's time to go downtown to the movie theater the record store clerk told me about. At least it would be something other than sitting around here bawling like a baby.

I'm going to go look in the newspaper and see if I can find out what's showing. As Porky Pig would say "Th-th-th-that's all folks!"

*August 24th*

*Dear Stevie,*

*You won't believe what I'm about to tell you, if you even get this at all.*

*We had a letter from Rusty, but it was dated last year. My mom is so upset. It appears to be the last letter he posted before he went missing. He talked about how bad things were, but in a joking manner* like, "It's so wet here all my socks have mold in them and now my toes are moldy, too." He said every time they have to cross a river they hold their weapons over their heads. But we already knew that, didn't we? We've seen it on the news more than once.

God. I'm praying he's alive and they just couldn't get the mail out, but Stevie, that letter makes me feel so sick inside.

I had to tell you.

I couldn't sleep last night after the letter came. I got out of bed and went out with the intention of visiting Buddy in the pasture, but instead I got in my car and drove halfway to the interstate. And then I had a flat tire.

It took me forever to change it because guess what? My spare was flat, too. And I know it wasn't flat before. I bought it off Skinny as soon as I got the 'Camino on my birthday.

I was coming to see you Stevie-girl. I needed to hear what you would say about that damn letter. (Sorry. Dang letter.)

But as usual, something got in the way. I would've been there by now if not for those two flats.

I walked six miles back to town in the middle of the night. Woke Skinny up and he came to the station and opened up, sold me a new spare, and drove me back out to where I'd left the 'Camino beside the highway.

That was an eerie walk, Stevie-girl. I kept

*thinking I heard things in the brush. Once I even thought I heard Rusty call my name. Stevie, you don't think this is his way of saying goodbye, do you? I'm so afraid he was being held captive by the NVA or even the Vietcong and now he's dead, so they mailed his letter just to get to us. I've heard they're cruel like that.*

*On the other hand, maybe Rusty managed to mail it himself—his spirit, I mean—the same way you said the lady-in-red took the letter right off Jonny Jensen's grave. I did finally get that letter from you, by the way. It just took a few extra days, which brings me back to my original thought.*

*Something prevented me from coming to Amarillo, Stevie-girl. My tires were just fine when I parked in front of my house after work. So how could they both go bad as soon as I headed to the Interstate?*

*Well, it doesn't really matter, does it? The fact is, I was headed there to see you, probably to beg you to come home, and it didn't happen. It turned out to be impossible.*

*I miss you like crazy, Stevie-girl. When I get ahold of you again, I am never ever going to let you go. Ever!*

*Sorry. I don't usually go on like this, (even if I think it all the time), but this thing with Rusty. This letter. It hurts. He said all he wants to do is get the hell out of there and come home, buy a fast car, and go to at least one more high school dance like he used to do. God. That guy loved to dance. Did I ever tell you that? There were dance parties nearly every weekend at our place, at his friend's houses, or sometimes at school. He loved to do the Twist. I can't get that image out of my head. Elvis Presley and Chubby Checker were his favorites. He would imitate the way they danced and he was just as good.*

*I don't know where he got that rhythm. I have two giant left feet. But you already know that from the Halloween dance we went to last year. I miss you, Stevie. Did I tell you that already?*

*Dad said my mom screamed when she saw the red white and blue AirMail envelope with Rusty's handwriting on it. He said he had to sit her on the couch before he could open it. He was afraid she was going to faint. I'm just glad he was home.*

*They didn't even call me at work.*

*When I got home, the two of them were still sitting on the couch, side by side, holding the letter between them. The pastor had come over and he was in the kitchen making phone calls to Rusty's recruiter up in Lubbock, trying to find out if he knew anything. But he didn't. He said he would find out if anything had changed and call back ASAP.*

*But of course, nothing had changed. There was no news at all. Can you believe it? We're right back to square one. No Rusty, no news. Just a year-old letter that made it sound pretty bad over there.*

*I did like you would have done, Stevie. I went to the library and started researching newspaper articles. I read everything I could find on the war. And on Vietnam in general. I especially researched battles that happened after Rusty was sent over. There was a terrible battle at a place called Dai Do. Rusty was there. 2nd Battalion/4th Marines, Golf Company. Oh, Stevie. Rusty was there.*

*Why can't they just tell us if he's dead? I don't want him to be dead, but this is awful. This is like purgatory. Oh, God, that was so selfish of me. Of course it isn't purgatory. It's not that hard on me, he's the one who might be lying in some lice-infested prison camp thousands of miles across the sea, probably feeling like his own country has forgotten about him.*

*Dammit. I've got to stop writing. This isn't doing anyone any good. I just can't stand the way this is affecting my family. Mom looks like a walking skeleton. She can't eat and doesn't even have an interest in church anymore. Not even her Bible Study group.*

*And on top of it all, I found out the reason my dad was home when the letter came is because his company is thinking of closing the Crossroads store and moving the inventory to Lubbock. He had come home to talk to Mom about just moving to Lubbock and taking the job as assistant manager there.*

*It seems like my parents can't catch a break. No wonder Dad's been so worried about money.*

*I don't know, Stevie-girl. I might chuck this letter in the trash and start over, the way you did the other day. But then again, I'm awfully tired. And I promised Skinny I'd open up for him*

*tomorrow (I've got to keep that promise consid-*
*ering how he came out and opened the station for*
*me in the middle of the night), so there you go. I*
*may or may not mail it, I just don't know.*

*At any rate, I miss you and I hope to see you*
*SOON!*

*Always yours,*

*Jase*

*P.S. That moon was huge in my windshield last*
*night. It painted a broad white stripe right up the*
*center of the hood of my El Camino. Then the tire*
*went flat. After that, I was too mad to notice. I can't*
*help but wonder how the moon looks over the rice*
*fields in Vietnam . . . or through the canopy of that*
*dense dark jungle.*

August 27th

Dear Jase,

You won't get this until I give it to you, but when I finally got a letter from you I sat right down on the couch and cried, then I began to write.

I'm so, so sorry about Rusty's letter. I'm not going to say I'm sorry about Rusty though because really, nothing has changed. It's only a letter. Probably it was carried around in some mail bag or something and forgotten until that guy discovered it underneath a pair of moldy old socks and thought, "Hmm, maybe I'd better mail this."

I know, I'm being silly, but it could happen. Lord knows we've seen our share of strange things so hey, don't lose hope, okay?

You won't believe the dream I had about a big blond bird. Be sure and remind me to tell you about it. I have a feeling I was dreaming it as you were fixing your flat tires on the Interstate.

By the way, I'm writing this from the road. Aunt Sophia put me on the bus this morning. I hugged her so tightly I thought I heard a rib crack (just kidding), and she hugged me right back. "I'll miss you," she said. "I hope you come back and visit every summer."

I couldn't even say anything my throat was so clogged up with feelings. I just nodded and hugged her again, and then I turned around and got on the bus before I could chicken out. Leaving Big Steve had been pretty bad. He held onto me for so long the guard came over and stood nearby.

"I'm sorry I have to get home," I told him. "School will be starting soon and I just can't stay any longer." I didn't tell him it was your letter that convinced me. What he doesn't know won't hurt him, right? Besides, I'd already made up my mind it was time. Your letter just gave me the strength to go on and tell him.

"I've kept you away from home too long," he said.

I shook my head and mumbled how much I would miss visiting him.

"I'm getting out of here, Stevie," he said. "The lawyer thinks I've got a good chance." His voice sounded almost strangled. I figured he was trying not to cry. I guess convicts don't cry in front of guards or something. "We'll be a family someday," he whispered. "I promise."

"I hope so," I told him. "But at least we can write letters now."

He squeezed me even tighter when I said that. To tell you the truth, I'm not sure we can ever be a family. What if he did get out? What if he came and wanted to change things, wanted me to leave Gramps and live with him? I couldn't do that. Gramps has always been my family . . . oh, here I go again, worrying about something that hasn't even happened yet.

Anyhow, it does make me sad to leave him. But it's a strange sadness, like a longing for something I lost rather than something I'm actually going to miss. Know what I mean? It's like I can't help but wonder what my life would have been like with a real father. But I know that's a stupid thought. I couldn't have had a better childhood. No way. So why should I feel sad?

I was still mulling it over when Aunt Sophia took my elbow and led me down the long hall, back through the double doors and out through the high, steel gates topped with razor wire. I wish I could show you a picture of this place, Jase, but we're not supposed to take photos of the outside walls. I guess they think we might use them to plan a jailbreak. Ha ha. My little attempt at humor. It's a dreary place, I'll tell you that much. Except in the sunshine, then it just looks sharp and dangerous.

In the parking lot, I began to tremble and sob. I couldn't help it. Aunt Sophia wasn't much better. She cried almost as hard as I did. Then we went straight to the bus depot. I had my overnight bag in the front seat and my suitcase in the backseat, all packed and ready.

Aunt Sophia is going to mail the paintings as soon as she gets home. I think she was waiting to make sure I really left. Before we went to visit Big Steve, we took my three paintings, wrapped them in padded brown paper, and tied them with string. Aunt Sophia kept the spring and winter landscapes in her den.

By the way, I've been thinking about it, and I think maybe the reason the German shepherd painting has remained untouched is because it's sort of a connection to you. Like maybe I'll need your help with all this, you know? Sort of like the *Field & Stream* pheasant. It was a connection and a clue, but I wouldn't have known about the magazine and the Arizona connection if it hadn't been for you. Everything seems to be tied together somehow.

Anyway, back to Aunt Sophia. She actually said I could stay and live with her and Uncle Burney if I wanted. I couldn't believe it. But it made me feel good, like now I have someone else I can depend on if something ever happens to Gramps (God forbid). And if Big Steve doesn't get out, although I don't really know how dependable he would be. (I hate to feel that way, but I can't help myself.)

Oh, Jase, I'm writing another novel here. Ha ha. I'm trying to get to the rest of it, to what happened after I got on that bus, but even my fingers seem to keep putting it off because well, because even for me it seemed unreal.

Okay, so I got on the bus in Amarillo and it pulled away from the curb. I turned to wave at Aunt Sophia, but she wasn't there. Instead, snow had begun to fall so fast and so hard that the entire bus depot had been obliterated. All I could see through the storm was a smear of red and I had to stop and try to recall if my aunt had been wearing her red jacket—I hadn't stained it or anything that day at the cemetery—but no, she was dressed in a sleeveless blue shell and white capri pants. According to the car radio, it had been almost one hundred degrees when we left the prison.

It was the phantom lady, Jase. She was standing on the bus platform in the falling snow. Let me correct that. She seemed to be standing there, but within seconds even the smear of red had disappeared, as the snowstorm became a sideways-blowing blizzard.

Wind howled around the black rubber door seal and the big bus rocked on its springs. I glanced over at the driver and it wasn't the brown uniformed man at all. It was the lavender clown with the purple derby. For the first time, I noticed a wilted daisy in the derby's hatband.

My heart thudded into the back of my throat. I've never been afraid of clowns, but how did he get out of the painting?

I'd checked it before we left—as we wrapped them in the brown paper—and the clown had been gone from the horse and sleigh and the regular black-jacketed man had been driving it again. Even the horse had turned its head back around, as if looking forward again. The other painting never changed back, though. It stayed all white with the black crash site in the center.

When I took it off the wall, snow had been falling just like now, sideways. Even the canvas felt stiff, frozen.

The wind howled again. The pneumatic doors groaned with the effort of keeping it out.

The clown began to turn his face toward me—I still hadn't even taken a seat—and when I saw his eyes, my whole body went numb and my suitcase fell to the floor with a thump. His eyes were silver, Jase, just like you said about the phantom pilot. They were two silvery orbs floating inside his head.

I grabbed for the big handle that controlled the doors, meaning to jump off and run back to the depot after Aunt Sophia, but the front of the bus disappeared in a puff of mist. The clown turned around, clicked his tongue against his teeth, and slapped the reins over the rump of the big black horse.

I fell backward into a seat that bounced as if on springs. Wintry air stung my face and I grabbed the furry blanket at my feet and wrapped it around myself.

The clown clicked his tongue and slapped the reins again and we were off, moving through the blizzard in a tiny bubble of fur-blanketed warmth.

And then you were there, Jase, moving alongside us in your cherry-red El Camino. I wanted to cry out, to tell you to stop and get me out of this crazy dream, but you just roared on ahead and were gone. Actually, I didn't see you at all, just your new car with someone's left arm resting outside the driver's window.

Then a voice said, "Are you all right, little lady?" And I

looked up into the face of the bus driver who wasn't a clown at all. But he did have a wilting daisy in his uniform lapel.

"I'm fine," I told him. "Just a little dizzy from the heat." And sure enough, I looked outside and the heat waves floated above the black asphalt ribbon of the road again.

I thanked him, picked up the bag I'd dropped, and started toward my seat. There were only about a dozen other people on the bus. "Where you headed, sweetie?" A woman with dark brown hair patted my arm. I hadn't even noticed her when I sat down in the aisle seat. It felt as if she'd appeared out of nowhere. I told her I was going home to Crossroads, and I asked her where she was going.

She said she was going home, too. Home to Winslow, Arizona.

Before I could even think, my instincts took over. "Winslow, huh? I've heard of that place. Big meteor crater there, right?"

The woman with the sweet smile nodded. "Oh, yes, Barringer Crater. It's quite amazing." A wistful look came into her eye. "I never knew my father, but he wrote me a letter before he died. He said the crater held a special place in his heart because when he was a little boy he wanted to be a scientist and study things like that—that's where the astronauts trained recently, you know." I nodded and she continued. "My father said living near the crater had made his imagination soar." Her voice cracked then, Jase. She hadn't been able to say anymore.

"Did he become a scientist?" I asked.

She shook her head sadly. "No." She pulled a dainty handkerchief from her purse. "He chose a different path, or I suppose I should say, it chose him. I never even got to know him. But oh, how I cherish that letter." She smiled at something in her memory. "It even had a funny little drawing of a clown on the envelope."

My heart almost stopped when she said that, Jase.

I held out my hand. "My name is Stevie Rae Sanders," I said. "I think you and I have a lot in common."

She grasped my fingers warmly. "Pleased to meet you, Stevie Rae Sanders. My name is Jean. But friends call me Stormy. Stormy Jean Jensen from Winslow, Arizona." She chuckled. "I was born during a snowstorm so bad Mama couldn't even get to the hospital. Had me at home, right there near that old crater."

I couldn't believe it. All the clues were coming together right here in the person of this sweet brown-haired woman. I wanted to jump up and down, or hug her neck. Or maybe both. Instead, I put on my best serious face and said, "Your poor mom, all alone in a storm, having a baby."

She laughed. "She wasn't completely alone. My two-year-old sister was there, too."

"Oh my, what an ordeal. No wonder you're named Stormy. If you don't mind my asking, where was your father, off at work or something?"

Her gaze went to the window, to the brown telephone poles whipping by outside. "No. He'd just been sent to prison for bank robbery. That's why we were all alone."

I couldn't say a word. No wonder the crater painting had filled with snow, obliterating the clown. It seemed to be the exact time he'd been wiped out of their lives forever. That could explain why Stormy's mother held such a grudge against her husband. "That must have been awful."

The woman patted my hand. "It was three days before anyone could get to us. Even the phone lines were down. They said we were lucky to be alive."

I tried to imagine the fear and pain Stormy's mother must have felt, but before I could say anything, she went on.

"The storm had a happy ending though—in a way. You see,

one of the policemen going door-to-door checking on people after the storm found us. He and my mother fell in love and got married. Turned out he was the best step-father a girl could ever want."

I couldn't keep the awe from my voice. "That's an amazing story." I bit my lip. "Do you mind telling me what happened to your mom?"

"Oh, we lost her last year. She was killed in a car accident." Her voice hitched again. "We buried her in her favorite red jacket. It was snowy that day. Such a moving sight, I'll never forget it."

I was dumbfounded. Her mom was killed in a car wreck, too. Had Big Steve even known she was dead? I didn't think so. Maybe Jonny Jensen didn't find out until he'd crossed over after his own death. No wonder the family never came for his things. His paintings. She had probably kept him a secret from everyone. But what about that letter Stormy says she received, who wrote that?

Jase, the similarities between my life and that of the Jensen family are so eerie it's like a parallel dimension or something. Maybe that's why the lady-in-the-red-jacket seemed to exist right there, but out of reach. Maybe that's where all spirits exist, in a parallel dimension.

I put my pencil down as the bus rocked along, lulling me to sleep. It has taken me this whole trip—in between naps—to write all this down.

But I haven't even gotten to the strangest part. You see after I woke (I guess I was exhausted), I excused myself and went to the bathroom at the rear of the bus.

That's when it finally occurred to me that Winslow is due west of Amarillo. Of course, I was headed to Crossroads, which was due south. If Stormy Jensen was going home, why she was on a bus headed the wrong direction?

I vowed to ask her.

I washed my hands and opened the narrow door. The bus was crammed with people. Had we made a stop while I was in the restroom? There'd been only about a dozen folks onboard when I went in.

Glancing out the window as I made my way up the black rubber runner leading to the front of the bus, I saw that the sun blazed overhead. High, white clouds dotted the horizon. Heat shimmered the very air around us.

There was only one empty seat on the bus, Jase. And sitting in it was my overnight bag. I couldn't find Stormy Jensen anywhere.

A man who appeared to be sound asleep with his head against the window occupied the seat beside my bag.

I glanced at the bus driver. His profile had changed, grown much smoother, unlined. From where I stood, I couldn't tell about the daisy in his lapel, but I knew in my heart it wasn't there. Somehow, I must have slipped into that other dimension (that's the only thing I can think of) and rode along with Stormy Jensen on her bus for a while.

I'm going to see her Jase. As soon as I can. Now that I know her name, I think I can find her again. And if you will help me, I hope to deliver those paintings in person. Then I can ask her if she's been on any trips lately. See if she remembers me from the bus.

I sat beside the sleeping man and stuffed my bag into the seat beside me. Fortunately, I don't take up that much space. When I woke a while later, my head had fallen over and made the overnight bag my pillow.

The man was awake. He glanced at me and smiled but didn't say anything. I felt completely disoriented not knowing how long I had slept or where we might be. A trail of drool ran from the corner of my mouth all the way to my ear on that side. I was embarrassed, but I figured it just showed how worn out I had become.

Opening my pack, I pulled out a thermos of chocolate milk and a bag of chips. I wanted the can of Coke Aunt Sophia had handed me at the last minute, but it felt warm. I should have poured it in the thermos and left the milk at home.

After my snack I stood and stretched. It was difficult to see out the bus windows unless I stood.

We appeared to be on I-20 not too far from home. Wow. I really had slept, or something. I'd somehow lost several hours.

All at once, a flash of red caught the corner of my eye.

It was your El Camino, for real this time. You kept pace with us for a few minutes, obviously trying to see in the windows, but since my seat was on the aisle, you couldn't see me and I couldn't see you.

When I saw that you were speeding up, I leaned over the no-longer-sleeping man and waved wildly.

"Friend of yours?"

I laughed. "That's my Jase."

The man slid over and let me have his seat. That's when I went crazy, waving and jumping around.

You honked your horn and stuck your hand out the window so that I could see it across the top of the car. You must've been watching for the bus back there at the roadside rest area. I figured you probably pulled out behind us when we passed.

I was surprised when you pulled even closer to the bus so that I could see inside the El Camino. That's when you leaned over and picked up something off the front seat and held it up so I could get a better view.

It was Sarey, my old hand-me-down rag doll. The one my gran had made for my mom when she was a little girl.

Tears sprang to my eyes. I was so moved that you had

remembered the one time I mentioned how I wished I'd brought Sarey with me to Aunt Sophia's house. I wiped away the tears. Sarey has been with me through thick and thin.

That's when I gave you that big thumbs-up.

You honked and waved goodbye, roaring on ahead of us toward town. I think my heart was thumping even faster than the motor in your new car.

The man sitting in my seat smiled and averted his eyes from my smeary face. I guess he thought I'd be embarrassed by my overwhelming emotions, but he was wrong. I was way too happy to be embarrassed. Seeing you made everything good again. Leaving Big Steve had felt like a small death, but now, I knew everything would be all right.

I don't know why I kept scribbling this letter to you. It seems once I started, I just couldn't stop.

I asked my seatmate if he wanted to switch places, back to where we were, but he shook his head and said he didn't mind. Then he asked if I lived in Crossroads and if you were my boyfriend and I said yes and then I asked if he lived in Crossroads, too. I knew I didn't recognize him.

He told me Crossroads wasn't his final stop that he would only get off to get a snack in the depot and then he would get right back on for the final leg of his journey to El Paso.

"That's a long way to go," I said. "It's right down on the Texas/Mexico border."

The man nodded. "But it's all worth it when you have a loved one waiting." His eyes twinkled and that's when my cheeks grew warm. I felt certain he was including us in that sentiment, Jase. You and me.

I have to stop writing now. We are pulling into the station. I will finish this tale in my diary tonight, in my own bedroom, in my own home, with Sarey in my arms, and Gramps in the living room watching the ten o'clock news. Maybe there will be something on there about the war. Maybe you will be sitting there with me, too. Maybe you won't go home until it's over and then I'll go to bed and write in my diary. We'll see.

It's so good to be home,

Just me,

Stevie-girl


Late that evening August 27th

Dear Diary,

Aside from a little more dust, the station hadn't changed one iota since I'd left it three months earlier.

I spied the El Camino right away. Jase was leaning back against the driver's side door, blond hair even blonder, streaked by the summer sun, and with that same unruly hank falling down over one eye. He had one long leg crossed over the other at the ankle, and he had one hand tucked into the front pocket of his blue jeans.

In the crook of that arm he'd tucked Sarey, my old doll.

He squinted into the late afternoon light as my bus bumped up the driveway entrance from the street. I got the impression he couldn't see into the bus from this angle. The westering sun seemed to bounce off our chrome right back into his eyes.

I studied him as we passed. He'd grown even taller. There was a distinct gap between the hem of his blue jeans and the tops of his sneakers. Just like him not to notice, I thought. Then I remembered what he'd said about financial difficulties at home.

The bus came to a stop near the doors and people stood up in the aisles and began taking their bags and boxes from the overhead compartments. I only had my overnight bag, which I'd held most of the trip, plus my suitcase, which Aunt Sophia had checked for me. It was stowed under the bus, so I'd have to wait to get it back.

My leg began to jitter up and down with the need to get up and get out, but the throng of people wasn't moving. A few folks remained in their seats, but most were jammed up in the aisle like vacuum-packed sardines.

I drew in a deep breath and sat back in my seat, counting backward from one hundred in an attempt to calm my nerves. It occurred to me that I hadn't seen Gramps, only Jase. But maybe he was already in the depot, waiting.

By the time I got down to thirty-five, the majority of the people were off the bus. I picked up my bag and walked to the door. My knees were weak as water.

Jase stood just outside the door with Sarey still tucked neatly under his arm. As soon as he saw me, he swiped the hank of hair off his forehead and smiled.

"You've grown." His voice held a note of awe.

I giggled. "I was about to say the same thing about you." I covered the distance between us in three easy steps and then he opened his arms (holding Sarey in one giant paw), and I stepped inside his embrace as if I'd never left.

"Oh, how I missed you," he whispered.

I hugged his middle and pressed the side of my face into his chest. "Me, too. So much."

We stayed like that for a moment and when I felt him loosen his hold, I stood back and looked into his eyes to see if everything was as I remembered.

It was. Exactly.

The blue of his iris was still like the sky, and his jaw was still as straight and sharp as a wooden ruler.

He leaned forward and brushed his lips against the top of my head. "You've gotten a lot taller. But I guess you'll never catch me."

I punched him lightly in the ribs and took Sarey from his grasp. "Thank you." I crushed her to me and breathed in her well-loved scent. "Where's Gramps? I thought he'd be here."

Jase stepped aside, flung his arm out in a grand, all-encompassing gesture meant to draw my attention to his new vehicle, and said, "He gave me permission to pick you up and deliver you safely home."

I walked over to the El Camino and touched it lightly. "Wow. It's gorgeous. You must wax it every day."

"She," he said. "It's a she. Her name is Red." I laughed. "Now that's original."

He blushed. But I didn't tease him anymore. "I've got a suitcase I need to get before we leave."

He took my bag and put it in the bed of the 'Camino. Then he held out his hand. I shifted Sarey to my other arm and placed my hand in his. It disappeared in his large warm palm and I sighed. It was so good to be home.

Glancing up as we crossed the parking lot back to where the driver was unloading the bus, I looked down at our hands and then up at his smiling face. The sun hovered low in the sky and it lit up his hair like a halo.

He winked and tweaked the end of my braid with his other hand.

"It's sure good to be home," I said.

Jase pulled me closer and we gently bonked our heads together the way we'd always done. Then he dropped my hand and ran to help the grunting driver who appeared to be struggling with an enormous bag that had become stuck in the compartment under the bus.

In minutes Jase and the driver had all the luggage unloaded onto the cart except for mine, which he had set aside when he pulled it out.

"Thank you, young man." The driver touched the brim of

his hat (not a purple derby I noticed) and stood up straighter, his hands immediately going to the small of his back. "I could use you at every stop." He grinned and Jase grinned back at him.

I felt my heart expand. My Jase. He always thought of others first.

"C'mon, Superman," I said. "I think we have time to go by A&W Drive-In for a root beer on the way home."

He turned and snatched me off my feet, twirling me in the air like I might've done Sarey if I'd been a ten-year-old boy with an ornery streak.

I squealed. "Put me down!" But in truth, I hoped he didn't.

Laughing, he carried me all the way to the El Camino. "I owed you that for keeping me in suspense with that letter."

I slid to the ground, my shorts hiking up in all the wrong places. "Okay, okay, now we're even." I swatted his shoulder as he bent to open the passenger door.

He ran back and grabbed my suitcase, depositing it in the bed of the vehicle with my overnight bag as I made all the necessary adjustments to my twisted clothing. That's when I noticed the packet of letters tucked into the console.

Jase climbed in beside me. "I haven't even got to read them all." He nodded toward the letters. "They got so mixed up in the mail. One of them just arrived today."

"That's wild," I said. "I've got one right here in my bag that I wrote on the bus. Once you read it, you'll know almost everything that happened."

"Almost everything?" He cocked an eyebrow at me. "Right now, I only know one thing." He started the El Camino and took a deep breath, staring straight through the windshield at the setting sun. "Some days I woke up unable to breathe because I was afraid you weren't coming back home."

"Jase—"

Before I could finish that thought. He leaned over, pulled

my face to his and kissed me tenderly. His breath was as sweet as Juicy Fruit gum.

"Never leave me again, you hear?"

I nodded and kissed him back, my lips encountering his chin instead of his lips. "I couldn't believe it when I saw you on the Interstate," I murmured. "I thought it would be Gramps."

His mouth whispered against my ear, "Disappointed?"

"Sure I am." I took his chin and pulled his face back to mine.

"Hold still, you." I placed my lips on his and kissed him soundly. "Now that you've got wheels, I'll never let you go."

The sun was nearly all the way down by the time we finished saying hello. "If we don't leave now, we won't have time for that root beer."

I sat up and straightened my clothing once again. "I know." I felt the heat creep back into my face. "But I don't care, do you?" Jase brushed my cheek with the pad of his thumb. "I'd stay just like this forever if it were up to me, but if your Gramps gets worried, he might not let you ride with me anymore."

"Good point. Home, Jeeves!"

He made a few clothing adjustments of his own and put the El Camino in reverse. As we drove through town toward the A&W, I told him everything that had happened—in the order in which it happened. And when I told him about riding along with Stormy, his mouth actually fell open as if unhinged.

I laughed at his expression. "I know, I know! First, her name is Stormy so I guess that's where the snowstorm fits in, but how I got on her bus, I will never understand."

We pulled up to a speaker at the A&W and Jase placed our order.

I filled in details for him while we waited on our floats, and within minutes, the carhop was there.

Jase handed me my drink, paid the girl, and told her to keep the change. Then he turned in his seat and just looked at me until I began to feel self-conscious.

"What is it?" I asked. "Do I have foam on my face?"

He laughed and reached across the seat for me. "Come here."

I slid over. I couldn't seem to get close enough. "I can't believe you're finally back."

I took a sip of my float to keep from having to respond. Truth was, I could hardly believe it myself. "Maybe we're just having the same dream or something." I grinned around my straw.

He tweaked my braid and wrapped both arms around me. "Stranger things have happened, ghost-chaser." He kissed me again, gently. "Hey, you still gonna go to work here next summer?"

I nodded. "Yep. Maybe even earlier if Gramps will let me work after school like you do."

"Maybe he will. If you mind your Ps and Qs that is."

I shrugged. "The only thing I'm worried about right now is whether those paintings make it here in one piece. I can't wait for you to see them."

Jase started the engine. "Yeah, me either. If I'd had my way, we would have brought them home with us when I picked you up in the 'Camino."

I leaned my head over on his shoulder. "It doesn't matter now. The thing I've got to figure out now is how to get the paintings to Stormy in Winslow."

Jase smoothed my hair and kissed the top of my head (I adored when he did that, for some reason it made me feel more loved than anything). "Let's see if we can find her in the phone book down at the library tomorrow. Then we can go from there."

I smiled. At the moment, I didn't care what happened with Stormy, or Jonny Jensen, or the-lady-in-red, or even my dad. For once, I was content just to be. Just to be snuggled up with my Jase in his new El Camino in the soft evening light of the A & W Drive In.

Diary, I'm going to close this entry soon. I'm so sleepy it isn't even funny. But if I don't make a note about the rest of that night, I might forget something important.

On the way home from the A & W, I asked Jase if there had been any more news about Rusty, but he said there hadn't. He said he didn't want to talk about it just then or it would ruin our evening.

To cheer him up, I remembered to tell him how the black shape that had hung around the cutoff to the prison seemed to have disappeared after I wrote that last note to Jonny. The one the lady-in-the-red-jacket took off his grave.

"Maybe you were right," Jase said. "Maybe you were able to lift the despair, or at least help it dissipate." He smiled in the muted light of the dash and it was a sad smile.

I wished I could find a way to lift the mantle of despair hanging over his family.

He drove me home and came inside to say goodnight to Gramps. It was like a fairy tale, parking at the curb and walking up to the front door hand-in-hand. Once again, I was struck by how tall he'd grown. I know that sounds stupid, Diary, since I seldom thought of anything else while I was gone, but it's true nevertheless.

Walking up the sidewalk with him gave me a feeling like I'd never had before. He'd changed in some minute way, or maybe I'd been the one who changed. It felt different, that's all I know. His jeans fit him differently, his feet no longer seemed in danger of tripping over each other, and he seemed quieter, more thoughtful, more... serious.

Probably that letter from Rusty, I thought. Well, that and working, driving, worrying, growing up while I was in limbo up in Amarillo.

As we neared the porch, my steps quickened. In seconds I'd broken from Jase and cleared the steps, flinging open the screen door and lunging through in one quick movement.

And there sat my Gramps, dozing in front of the TV.

As soon as I saw him, guilt flooded my senses. I should have come straight home from the bus station instead of lollygagging around with Jase. I fell to the floor at his feet and told him those exact words.

But Gramps just squeezed me and chuckled. I had both my arms around his neck by then. "Young love," he said. "No one can stand in its way."

I hid my face against him when he said that. Gramps had always been a teaser. "I'm just glad to be home."

He chuckled again and I helped him stand.

We all made our way to the kitchen table where I regaled them with photos and news of my dad and Aunt Sophia, Uncle Burney—of which there was very little—and even the lady-in-red.

I half-expected Gramps to try and debunk my theory about Jonny Jensen and the woman-in-red, but he didn't bat an eye. He'd been partially involved when we solved the mystery of the phantom student the year before.

"We should be getting the paintings in a couple of days. Aunt Sophia said she couldn't wait to get them out of her house." I looked at the two of them. "I think they gave her the creeps."

Gramps leaned back in his chair. "Quite a story," he said. "I can't wait to see them." He rubbed his gnarled old chin with his forefinger. "Gotta tell ya, though. If the spirits are that strong—strong enough to pierce the veil—we may not have those pictures for long."

"What do you mean? They might self-destruct or something?"

Gramps stood and made his way to the refrigerator. "I'm thinking we might have to make a road trip . . ." I saw a tiny twitch of his lips just before he leaned down and stuck his head in the fridge.

I glanced at Jase.

His hand shot up as if we were both back in Mrs. Boyd's class in elementary school. "I'll drive!" he said.

I couldn't help it, I laughed out loud.

His face turned pink and he put his hand down, but he smiled, too.

"First we have to go to the library tomorrow and see if we can find her address."

Gramps pulled out the milk and I immediately got up and retrieved the yellow box of Nestle's Quik chocolate powder from the cupboard.

We all enjoyed a glass of chocolate milk even though two of us had just had root beer floats.

Gramps patted his middle. "I'm about done in."

I knew that was his way of saying it was bedtime. "Yeah," I agreed. "I've got to unpack my suitcase."

Jase jumped up as if launched. "I left it in the 'Camino." He hurried out of the kitchen.

"Have you seen his new car?"

Gramps nodded. "Came around first thing, lawn mower in the back, took me for a ride." He grinned. "Darn good driver, too. Only reason I let him go down to the station and pick you up." He stood and stifled a yawn with his fist. "Sure is good to have you home, Stevie-girl." He indicated the door with a nod of his head. "I'm going on to bed. Lock up soon, now."

I stood and wrapped my arms around him again. "I will, Gramps. It is *so* good to be home."

He patted my head and clucked. Then he gave me another squeeze and walked down the hall toward the bathroom. In a minute, I heard the water running and Gramps humming. His rendition of "Farther Along" was like the icing on the coming-home-cake. It meant all was right in my little corner of the world.

Jase came through the front door with my suitcase and my overnight bag.

"Thanks." I took them from him. "Gramps is getting ready for bed."

Jase held out his hand. "Wanna walk me out?" I nodded and took his hand. "Is the moon up?"

He laced his fingers through mine. "It sure is."

We stepped out onto the porch and gazed up at the night sky. The white orb appeared almost full. The shadowy man-in-the-moon face smiled down.

"That's ours," Jase said. "Our moon." He pointed toward the stars. "And there's the North Star. Just like always."

I squeezed his hand as he pulled me into his side and kissed the top of my head. I raised my face and waited. He pressed his lips to mine and I stood on tiptoe to touch his hair and the back of his neck. Only later did I wonder if any of the neighbors were watching. But in that moment, the only thought in my head was Jase and how good it was to be home so we could stand under the North Star—together—in our very own patch of moonlight.

. . .

August 31st

Dear Diary,

Aunt Sophia must have put a rush on the paintings. I guess she really did want to get rid of them. They arrived by post within three days just like our regular letters had *usually* done.

That did it. As soon as Gramps and Jase saw the paintings, both agreed they needed to be given to Stormy Jensen immediately. We had just over a week of summer before the start of the new school year.

Skinny gave Jase a few days off for what he called one last summer hurrah. I liked the sound of that. In fact, I couldn't wait to hit the road with my two best guys. Now, we just had to convince Jase's folks. Don't forget, Diary, they didn't know all the spooky things we knew. Gramps only knew a little bit, but it was enough to convince him his original "road trip" idea had been a good one.

"I've got a burr under my saddle anyway," he'd said. "A bit of wanderlust calling."

We were eating watermelon on the back porch at the time. "Wanderlust?"

He spit a black seed halfway across the yard. "Yep. Happened after I got out of the hospital. You were gone and the Widow Conner kept coming around like I was some kind of invalid or something. Made me realize maybe I don't have that much time left."

"Oh, Gramps . . ."

"'Sides all that, I've never seen the Grand Canyon." He took another bite of watermelon. "Always meant to. Heck, I saw Europe on the Army's dime, but I never seemed to have time to see all the sights in our own amazing country."

I jumped up and hugged his neck. "After that, maybe we can see the Statue of Liberty."

That got him so tickled he almost choked on a seed. Slapping his knee, he said, "Stevie-girl, it's a long way from Arizona to New York City."

So that's how it came to be that four days after I got home from Amarillo, the three of us were piling into Jase's El Camino at dawn, headed to Winslow.

A couple of days before, Gramps had showed us the tiny area code map in the front of our local phone book (all of Arizona had area code 602) and then he instructed us how to call the long distance directory assistance operator for that area (1-602-555-1212).

Sure enough the operator was able to give us both the phone number and the street address for Stormy Jensen. I couldn't believe how easy it was to locate her once we had her name and city. Thank goodness Stormy didn't have an unlisted number. That would have been a whole other ballgame.

I hadn't slept a wink after the paintings arrived and we made the decision to go. When Jase drove me to the post office to pick them up, we'd wanted to rip the paper off right there in the El Camino, but we had taken a deep breath, and waited. I really wanted to open them with Gramps. It seemed important that he share in the unveiling.

Back at home my hands were shaking when I reached for the corner of the heavy postal tape. The paintings had been cradled in slim wooden frames and covered in an outside layer of manila-paper-bubble wrap. "Must have cost Aunt Sophia a fortune to mail these," I remembered saying. "Didn't we wrap them in brown paper before we left?" I shrugged. "I guess the post office made her do it this way, but still, what if they're damaged? Or different than I recall?"

Jase had rubbed his palms together comically. "C'mon, Stevie, the suspense is killing me."

"Okay." I pulled a bit of the tape. "Here goes . . ." Gramps had leaned forward, elbows on his knees.

I peeled the paper back slowly. Under the padding, the wooden cradle-frames were held together with tiny screws. "We need a small Phillips screwdriver."

Jase jumped up and ran toward the kitchen. Then he turned back and stood in the doorway. Swiping the white-blond hank of hair off his forehead, he glanced at the floor, then at me. "I – uh, I sort of assumed you'd have one in the kitchen junk drawer like we do at home."

Gramps chuckled. "Must be a universal law." He waved his hand toward the kitchen. "Third drawer to the left of the sink."

Jase grinned. In seconds he was back with the screwdriver.

We unwrapped the paintings in silence. The first one to emerge had been the German shepherd.

"Ahhh," Jase sat back on his heels. "Lady." I touched his sleeve. "I know."

He nodded. I don't think he could say anything else right then.

Gramps reached for the second painting. They were all the same size, 18"x24" (standard prison canvas size I suppose), so I didn't have a clue whether the clown would be staring out, or if it would be the black horse pulling the sleigh.

I unwrapped it in silence. The horse pulling the sleigh through the drifted snow became visible. I'd forgotten how the trees all appeared to have beards of pure white. "I love this one." I held it up for Jase and Gramps to see. "But for a while, the driver had changed to the purple clown and the beautiful black stallion had turned his head to look behind him. At me." I heard my voice wobble when I said that last part. I couldn't help it.

Gramps' mouth turned down at the corners, but he didn't say

anything. I think most folks would have wanted to correct me, to say that can't be true, but not my Gramps. He trusted me. Jase took the painting and stood it against the wall so we could all see it properly. "It's beautiful. A Christmas card, like you said."

I bit my lip, reached for the last painting. "This is the one." I looked at Gramps. "This is the one that gave me such fits." I pulled up the tape and tore off the bubble-wrap-paper before Jase could even finish removing the screws at the corners.

All the breath escaped my lungs in a whoosh. It was just as I remembered.

"It started out as a white-faced clown wearing a purple derby," I explained. "Now, it's just this – this hole in the ground."

"Crash site," Jase said. "Barringer Crater." "Meteor Crater?" Gramps asked.

I nodded. "We think it's the Barringer Crater near Winslow, where Stormy Jensen lives."

Gramps leaned forward a bit more. "It's snowing."

Jase bent forward, too. "Wow. Just . . . wow." He sat back on his heels and looked at me. "I know you told me, but still, it's just . . . wow."

I reached out to touch the painting. It felt dry, and yet we could clearly see feathery little flakes floating down from the painted sky, softening the dark center with snow.

"Back in Amarillo, this snow blew sideways, like a blizzard, like urgent. Now, it seems much gentler."

"Not so urgent," Jase agreed. "More of a reminder than a demand."

I took a good, deep breath. "I think you're right. As if it's telling us we're on the right path, just not there, yet."

"The path," Gramps said. "The journey." He motioned

toward the other painting, the horse pulling the sleigh down the woodland path.

"Gee, Gramps. You catch on quick. I never even thought—"
"Hah!" He leaned back in his chair. "Quite a tale." He slipped his hankie from his overall pocket and mopped his upper lip.
"I'd say we definitely need to call Ms. Stormy Jensen. See if she even wants us to head on over to Winslow, Arizona."

I jumped up and hugged his neck. "Thanks, Gramps. You, me, and Jase, right?"

Gramps nodded. "We can share the driving, if Jase doesn't mind. That way we can stay on the road longer, get there sooner."

Jase looked down at his feet. "We – uh. We can take the 'Camino. There isn't a whole lot of room, but Stevie doesn't take up much space." He grinned, thinking, perhaps, of having me beside him in the seat like we were when he picked me up from the bus depot. I know I was certainly thinking about it—of course I was thinking about my Gramps being there, too, but you take what you can get, right?

"I'll call your folks after I talk to Ms. Jensen," Gramps said. "We don't want to get our cart before our horse, so to speak."

We all glanced at the painting of the horse and sleigh, and then sat by while Gramps called the number the operator had given us.

I held my breath as we waited for someone to answer the phone in Arizona.

Gramps was quite the diplomat. He patiently explained the situation about Big Steve and the paintings and at first it sounded as if Stormy Jensen didn't believe it—or so it seemed from our side of the conversation—but then she appeared to relent. After a few moments, Gramps grinned and gave us the thumbs-up.

I waited until I was outside, walking Jase to his vehicle, before I jumped up and down. "It will be so cool, won't it?"

He nodded and looped an arm around my shoulders. "We have to do it. I mean, that crater painting is downright freaky. Did you see your Gramps' face when you unwrapped it?"

"Yeah, yours, too. I know I told you about it, but—" "—seeing is believing. I know. It looks really strange."

He stopped walking and stood as if in thought. "I can see why you didn't want to leave. This spirit is strong, but is it Jonny Jensen's spirit, or the lady-in-the-red-jacket?" He seemed to think about what he'd said. "Or could it be both?"

Before I could answer, he said, "Whatever, or whichever one it is—or was—they weren't trying to scare you away, they were trying to keep me away. Trying to keep me from coming up there and bringing you home."

I squeezed his waist in a self-conscious sort of hug and watched as he folded his lanky frame into the low-slung El Camino. "Have a good day at work." I giggled when I realized how funny that sounded—like a TV sitcom wife or something.

"You, bet, June. I'll see you for dinner tonight."

I slugged his shoulder through the open window. "Oh, you're evil."

He laughed and drove away holding his hand over the spot where I'd slugged him. "I'll call you later, Slugger. Try to stay out of trouble between now and then."

I tilted my chin up, spun on my heel, and flounced back into the house. I loved teasing and being teased by the two men in my life.

When I got back inside, Gramps was hanging up the phone. "I just talked to Jase's Dad."

I raised my eyebrows. "What'd he say?"

"After a little discussion, he agreed. It seems they are having a rough time right now—"

"The letter?"

"You knew about that, huh?"

"Yeah, Jase was pretty upset about it, but not nearly as much as his mom, I'll bet. I remember when she first found out Rusty had gone missing—it was bad, I didn't know if she was going to survive that news."

Gramps frowned. "On top of that, they're moving to Lubbock in a few months."

My heart fell into my stomach. "What?"

He nodded. "Sorry. I thought you knew that, too."

I shook my head. "Jase said his dad's company *might* close the branch store here, but he never said they were definitely moving." My knees buckled, and I sat down on the nearest chair. "I can't imagine Crossroads without Jase."

Gramps rocked on the balls of his feet the way he always did when he was thinking. "It would be a shame to make the boy move when he's doing so well in school and with his new job."

I chewed at the cuticle around my thumb. Something I hadn't done in ages. "Maybe things will change and they won't go."

"Reminds me of when I met your Gran . . ." He hitched at his overalls and went off into the kitchen. I wanted to ask more, but figured if he wanted to tell me, he would. Sitting out on the back porch at the end of the day was our best time for "conversatin'" as he called it. Maybe he would tell me then.

But Diary, we didn't have much time to "conversate" that evening. The Widow Conner came over and brought us an apple pie. I walked down to the Piggly Wiggly, got a bag of rock salt, and some heavy cream and Gramps got out the ice cream maker. We took turns cranking the handle and I told Gramps how much faster it would go if Jase had been there to crank. That really made him laugh, but he admitted it was true.

And I had to admit that the Widow Conner made absolutely the best apple pie I'd ever tasted, except for my Gran of course. But that just goes without saying.

After the pie, we played a few hands of gin rummy and I'm ashamed to say it pleased me when Gramps and I won them all. The Widow didn't win a single hand. It was both surprising and quite satisfying. I kept expecting Gramps to let her win the way he used to let me win from time to time, but he never did.

Jase called me on his supper break around six-thirty and I took the phone with its extra-long curly cord and slipped into the hall closet where the water heater lived. It's the same way I'd always talked to Karla when she still lived down the street. The two of us would be on the phone for hours unless we were sitting out in the front yard together. Now, I automatically did the same thing when Jase called.

"It's so nice to be able to talk to you on the phone again," I said when I got comfortable.

"Yeah, I missed that, too. But I enjoyed your letters. All except the one about the music store clerk."

I laughed but didn't tell him he had nothing to worry about. Maybe a little self-doubt was a good thing. Sometimes it seemed as if Jase was almost too good to be true. Mama used to tell me if something seemed too good to be true, then it probably was. Or maybe that was just my own self-doubt kicking in. I kept waiting for him to get tired of me, to decide he wanted someone like the girl Karla had become after she moved to California. Someone more experienced. More exciting.

"Anyhow," Jase paused, took a sip of something, "whatever your Gramps said to my dad did the trick. He said he doesn't mind if I help drive to Winslow. He even offered me his Pontiac, but then he remembered he had to use it to take some of the company big wigs to lunch one day."

"So it will be Gramps' pickup or the El Camino, then?"

Jase laughed and it sounded like his mouth was full. "The 'Camino. Old Red rides pretty smooth, don't you think?"

"Yes, I do." I couldn't *not* agree, it would have broken his heart. Besides, I didn't care what we were driving as long as I got to sit in the middle beside him.

"Well, all right," he said in his best Buddy Holly imitation. "I've been looking at the map, you know Skinny has a whole rack of roadmaps here, and I judge it will take us twelve to four-teen hours to get there, allowing for a break now and then."

I gulped. "I hope Gramps can do that. It sounds kind of tiring."

"We can break it up into shorter periods," Jase said. "It just means we have to stop and spend the night somewhere . . ." His voice trailed away for a moment, then he said, "Hey, we could take camping gear."

I tried to picture my Gramps camping and while we had done it a time or two over the years, fishing and camping, I didn't know if it was a good idea since he'd had the heart attack. "Let me talk it over with him. After the widow leaves."

Jase made a funny little laugh, like one he'd tried to stifle at the last minute. "The Widow Conner, huh?"

I told him about the pie and the ice cream and the game of rummy.

"Dang," he said. "I sure wish I had been there. Homemade ice cream is my favorite food in the whole world."

"Want me to get on my bike and bring you some?"

He stayed silent for a few seconds. "Nah, it would just melt. But save me a bowl in the freezer, okay?" I promised him I would.

"I'll be there to get y'all in the morning. I think we need to leave as early as possible."

"Sounds good to me . . . as long as Gramps has no objections." We hung up after I heard the distinctive *b-r-r-r-n-g* that meant a car had just run over the alarm hose signifying a customer at the gas pumps.


The alarm went off at four o'clock and I made three scrambled egg sandwiches on toast. Jase arrived and came right on inside, led by the delicious smell, or so he said.

We ate quickly, and after he was done, Jase reached into the freezer with a slightly embarrassed grin and retrieved his bowl of ice cream. He ate it standing at the kitchen sink with a look of pure bliss on his handsome face.

Gramps told us he thought camping out would be a fine idea if we would let him take his old Army cot so he didn't have to sleep on the ground. We had discussed it briefly the night before, after Widow Conner finally went home.

Jase quickly agreed. "And if all else fails, I think there are some teepees somewhere along Route 66."

We all laughed at that, but I was pretty sure I'd seen pictures of them, too. I just couldn't remember where. It may have been in *Life* magazine, or *Reader's Digest*. I always read them down at the library, and last year Gramps got me my very own subscription to *Reader's Digest* for my birthday. I love the true stories called *Drama in Real Life*. Now it comes in the mail, every month, just like clockwork. Maybe I should be a writer, too, a writer of nonfiction. I do love doing research.

At last, we loaded up the El Camino and took off. I felt like Alice in Wonderland. What wondrous surprises awaited us? There were certain to be some strange things in store, given that we were following the cryptic advice of spirits in order to deliver the paintings of a dead bank robber to his unwitting daughter.

Heading west was great. The morning was fresh and clean. There wasn't another car on the road. My tiny hometown was sleeping as snugly as the proverbial bug in a rug.

"This is nice," Gramps said. "A journey should always be started early in the morning." He smiled and adjusted his side mirror to catch the rising sun. "Look at those colors." His voice was filled with awe. "Sunrises and sunsets. My favorite times of the day." He turned on our main road to head down toward the highway out of town. "Thanks for letting me drive first," he told Jase. "My old eyes aren't what they once were, the earlier it is, the less traffic, less glare, too."

"I understand," Jase said. "Just drive as long as you want, then I'll take the wheel."

I smiled, wondering once again, if my best buddy was too good to be true. And my Gramps! How many other kids could convince their grandpas to take off across the country on the advice of a phantom?

Don't look a gift horse in the mouth my subconscious said (another of Gramps' sayings). So I gave up wondering about my good fortune and took my skinny feather pillow and wedged it in between my head and Jase's shoulder.

I closed my eyes, dozing on and off, listening to the sound of Gramps' voice as he related how he'd met Gran and married her when she was sixteen and he was eighteen. I had a feeling it was the story he'd been about to tell me on the back porch a couple of days earlier.

"We were set up on a barn dance date by her daddy. She always said he just wanted to get rid of her and I was the nearest boy around. It was the Great Depression, you know. She had eight siblings and not too much food." His voice grew soft. "I married her and took her to California. She went to work in a factory soldering wires inside radios while I picked grapes and other fruits." He pulled the brim of his cap down lower. "On her days off from the radio factory, she came out to the vineyards and worked right alongside me."

"Wow. Just like *The Grapes of Wrath.*"

Gramps laughed. "Maybe not just like that. But yes, when your mama was born, we were living in a workers camp in the San Joaquin Valley."

"I remember Mama talking about it. She said she spent all day playing with the other camp kids. She also said it was the best place in the world to grow up, except for the bears that came down at night to raid the garbage dump."

Gramps nodded. "That was something all right. But most of us pickers were too tired to worry about a few hungry bears. We just taught the kids to come in at dusk, then we let the bears scavenge."

"You said you saw Europe on the Army's dime?" Jase's voice sounded tight.

"That I did," Gramps replied. "Oldest man in my outfit." He sighed, but it wasn't a contented sigh. It was inexplicable. "When Japan hit Pearl Harbor, I enlisted." He patted my knee. "Sent your mom and gran home on the bus, then after basic, I shipped out to Europe."

We waited a few minutes, but no more information was forthcoming. I could tell Jase wanted to ask more about the military. About being listed as MIA, or being captured, perhaps. About the treatment of POWs, most likely, but he didn't ask. Maybe he didn't know how. Or maybe he was afraid to find out. After a long pause, Gramps murmured. "The boys in my outfit called me Pop. I wasn't really old enough to be their dad, but I was old enough to be their big brother, or their uncle, maybe." He paused, and I felt as if he were giving Jase the perfect opening.

Still, he didn't take it.

So I did. "Hey, Gramps . . ."

"Hey, Stevie-girl . . ."

I almost giggled, but the question was too serious. "Did anyone in your outfit get killed, or you know, captured?"

For a minute, I didn't think he would answer. Finally, he said, "We lost a lot of good men. Some were captured. Hitler didn't take many prisoners, though."

As usual, I spoke without thinking. "What happened to them? The ones who survived?"

Gramps focused on his driving. "They were sent to prisoner of war camps. In Germany they called them stalags. Thanks to the Geneva convention, most of the POWs were treated much better than the concentration camp prisoners." He stopped talking but I sensed he wasn't finished. "Not so, in the Japanese POW camps, though. Thankfully I wasn't in the Philippines or that theater. Those guys were badly abused."

"The Bataan Death March," Jase muttered. "We read about it in History."

"That, and more . . ." Gramps replied.

Jase took a deep breath. "Do you think it's that bad in Vietnam?"

"Son," Gramps said, "there's always hope—"

"I keep hearing on the news about The Hanoi Hilton, I think it's a sarcastic name for one of the worst prisoners of war camps. I read about a man named Jerry who blinked the word torture in Morse code when they made him appear before a camera—"

"I've read about that one, too." Gramps reached along the seat behind my head and clasped Jase by the shoulder. "Give it to God," he said. "Just give it all to God, let him worry about it."

I felt Jase begin to shake. Trying to stifle sobs, I thought.

Gramps squeezed his shoulder and gave it a few pats, then

he left his palm there and I felt Jase settle like his horse Buddy after a hard gallop.

We drove on through the day—with stops for gasoline and snacks along the way—and by suppertime we were nearing Arizona. As soon as we crossed the border we saw the first teepee campground. The teepees were actually made of concrete and seemed more like an odd motel than a campground, but still, it was different. We all agreed we had to stop. I shared a teepee with Gramps—twin beds—and Jase had his own teepee across the courtyard.

It was so cool. The cone-shaped rooms all formed a circle around a larger teepee that housed the office and the restaurant. After we stowed the paintings and our overnight bags in our "rooms," we met up in the café and had a great supper of club sandwiches and iced tea. We even had fried ice cream for desert. That was a first for me. (It was delicious. At first I thought it was a joke of some sort, but the waitress finally convinced me it was a real menu item, and after that, we all had to have a bowl).

The drive couldn't have been better, except for the pall of Jase's brother Rusty. I got absolute chills after hearing Jase recount the story of the POW who blinked t-o-r-t-u-r-e in Morse Code so our government would realize the words he was being forced to say were not true.

I made Jase tell me more about it after they changed drivers and Gramps fell asleep against the passenger door.

In reality, the government discovered our captured soldiers were being hogtied and hung up on meat hooks from the ceiling, beaten, starved, and tortured by numerous other methods—one called The Ropes—that sounded like something straight out of the Middle Ages. No wonder Jase and his parents could hardly concentrate on anything other than Rusty. I'd be worried sick, too.

Of course, it was possible he wasn't a Prisoner of War at all. He could be dead and his remains unfound or unidentified. It seemed none of the possibilities were good, but I told Jase my theory that Rusty might have been injured and was simply lying in a military hospital somewhere, in a coma perhaps, unable to communicate, unable to tell them his name. I know, I know, a soldier's dog tags are supposed to be their identification in cases like that, but dog tags can get lost, can't they?

If I ever do get to communicate with a spirit, in real time instead of a beat late like it usually occurs, I'm going to ask that spirit to find out about Rusty. If he's no longer on this earth then the spirits should know, right? Sounds logical to me, unless I really stop to think about it. I mean if they have to have the assistance of a kid like me, then they must not know much on either side of the veil.

I wonder if séances really work? They scare me for some reason. Helping a lost phantom is one thing, attempting to conjure one out of thin air is something else entirely. Think I'll leave them alone. No use asking for trouble. I get into enough of that without even trying.

I finally fell asleep wishing we were camping in a real teepee instead of one made of concrete. Try as I might, I couldn't hear any wildlife through those thick walls, not even a cricket. Of course, Gramps' snoring didn't help, either. It was like sleeping in the same room as a logger testing his new chainsaw.

The next morning, we were up with the sun again. When I'd finished dressing and peeked out the window, Jase stood at the railing that surrounded the campground.

On the other side of the rail fence were actual tent and RV sites. Watching him for a moment, I sensed that he was holding himself very still. Following his probable line of sight, I soon saw what had piqued his interest.

In a small clearing between a low stand of mesquites and a towering saguaro stood a good-sized javelina and half a dozen piglets.

I'd seen one or two javelina on the hiking/camping trips I'd made with Gramps down in Big Bend, but I'd never seen babies before. Like all young animals, they were awfully cute. But when I stepped out and Jase turned to wave, the sudden movement startled the wild family. Mom snorted and trotted off into the thicker brush. The babies followed obediently, single file all the way.

Jase grinned. We shared a love of wild things and the outdoors. I was glad we'd shared this little scene, too, even if it was only for a moment.

We were in Arizona, now. That meant we had a couple more hours driving time and then we'd be there, at Stormy Jensen's house. It felt surreal, like surfacing from a long, strange dream.

Jase came and took my hand, pressed his lips to the top of my head. I squeezed his fingers and together we got Gramps and strolled back to the big teepee where we shared a leisurely breakfast of bacon and eggs in the quaint café.

"Be there by noon." Gramps buttered his toast with loving strokes. When he glanced up and caught me staring, he smiled. "The Widow Conner discourages the use of too much butter." He tapped his chest. "On account of the old ticker, you know."

I nodded. "Good for her." I wanted to take the little pat of butter away—he'd gone to work on his second slice of toast— but he was still my Gramps. My boss. So, I stayed quiet. In a moment, he pushed it aside all by himself. "Darn that woman."

Jase laughed and that got me giggling. "Like my mom," he said. "Even when she isn't here, she's always here." He tapped his temple.

Gramps huffed. "Parents, yeah. They're supposed to get in your head. Old Widow ladies, that's a horse of a different color."

Then he pointed his butter knife at me. "And don't go telling her I called her an old horse."

I laughed out loud. "I wouldn't dream of it. She might never make us another apple pie if I told her that."

Gramps snorted laughter. "Good point." Then he dug into his breakfast with great relish.

Jase and I followed suit and in less than an hour we were finished and packed up, ready to complete this journey and get back to real life once more.

Before we left, Gramps went to the office and placed a call to Stormy Jensen to let her know we were almost there. He had the operator reverse the charges so he could pay for it with our motel room bill.

"I hope she likes us," I said. "Although I guess it doesn't really matter, after today we'll probably never see her again."

"She's excited," Gramps replied. "She can't wait to meet us and see the paintings her father intended for her to have. She said she has wondered about him her whole life. Apparently her mom let them think he was dead."

I nodded, remembering how Gramps had said basically the same thing to me in regards to Big Steve and his letters. "I guess that's one reason he never had visitors."

Jase took my hand as we walked across the lot to the El Camino. "It amazes me that people can let go of each other so easily." He dropped my hand and slipped his arm around my shoulders. "I could never do that, not in a million years."

I leaned into his side. Thank you, Jase. Thank you for saying that. I felt certain he was referring to the existence of my own dad, which had been a complete mystery until the night of Gramps' heart attack.

After we grabbed our gear, and the paintings, we climbed back into the El Camino and drove on down the road.

"If we wrap this up quickly, we'll have time to stand at the edge of the Meteor Crater and the Grand Canyon." Gramps tilted his head to the side and swiped a hand over his thinning white hair. "They aren't that far apart, you know."

"That sounds great." I patted his knee the way he usually did mine.

Jase began to whistle a tune. Try as I might, I couldn't make it out, and then he got to the refrain and I recognized "The Long and Winding Road" by the Beatles.

That's when we saw the sign for the Petrified Forest. I was intrigued.

"Put it on the list for the way back," Gramps said. "Shouldn't take but a few minutes to see a forest of stone."

We laughed and drove on.

The landscape amazed us into complete silence.

Then we passed the sign for Window Rock. "Hey, isn't that on the Navajo Indian Reservation?"

"Sure is," Jase said.

I reached into my pocket where the chunk of turquoise rested. It seemed everything was beginning to come full circle, but of course the real test was yet to come.

We drove on through the growing heat of the morning. Arizona seemed a lot like my own home state. Even though summer was ending, and the new school year about to begin, the seasonal warmth wasn't through with us yet.

After a few more miles, we began to see signs about the crater. I knew we were getting close, and then the sign for Winslow popped up and Jase looked at me and smiled.

My knee began to jump. When he put on the turn signal for the exit, Gramps laid his palm on my knee to calm it. I put my hand on top of his. "I can't wait to see the Grand Canyon after this," I said.

He nodded. "Me, either, kiddo."

The air was dry and the clouds were just rumors of white

marching across the horizon. No one said much of anything until Gramps murmured, "I think this is the street. Look, there's our turn."

And then we were there, driving through a neat neighborhood of family style homes with open yards and few trees.

Jase pulled up to the curb and stopped. "Well," he said. "I think this is it."

We all studied the single story home. It was tan and white with a nice sized porch and a deep overhang.

Jase was the first to exit the car.

He held the door open for me. Both my knees were shaking like fall leaves in a good breeze. Gramps climbed out and stood beside the 'Camino, hands pressed into the small of his back, reminding me of the Greyhound bus driver back at the station that day.

He stretched and groaned while Jase took the paintings out from under the protective tarp in the bed of the vehicle.

We all paused beside the mailbox, checking the address one last time, before walking up to the neat little house with the wide, wide porch.

I stopped once, to readjust my grip on the purple clown painting. It was still done up in brown paper and bubble wrap, of course, but I had marked it with the letter P so I would know. Jase carried the German shepherd, which I'd marked with a D for dog. It was also wrapped in brown paper.

Gramps came behind us carrying the winter scene, the one of the mysterious sleigh being pulled by a black horse.

Jase let me climb the porch steps first. I watched my finger go toward the bell as Gramps stepped up behind us. I wondered what Stormy Jensen must think if she happened to be peering at us out the window, or through the peephole in the door.

After pushing the bell, my hand went into my pocket where my fingers located the lump of turquoise. I rubbed it for luck, for comfort. I wasn't sure if I should offer it to Stormy, or whether I should keep it for myself. It was given to me as a link, a clue from Jonny or from the lady-in-the-red-jacket (I wasn't sure which). Maybe I didn't want to give that up, yet. After all, my own father was still there, still in prison, not far from Forever Field. Maybe I'd better hold onto my talisman a while longer, for my dad's sake.

After rubbing the turquoise, my hand went to my throat to feel for the chain holding my new locket. The one Big Steve had draped over my head on our last visit. It held the tiny picture of mom and me, and now a new photo of my dad enclosed in the opposite frame.

As I stood rubbing the necklace, thinking of Big Steve, the door opened and there stood Stormy Jean Jensen. She was shorter than I thought she'd be, but it's hard to tell someone's height when they are sitting in a bus seat.

Behind her, on the wall in what I assumed was the living room, hung a portrait of a beautiful woman. I knew right away it was Stormy's mother; she even had on her favorite red jacket. A tall, handsome man in a police uniform stood beside her in the portrait. I assumed it was her stepfather, the one who had found and rescued them after the storm.

I held out my hand. "Hello. I'm Stevie." I introduced her to Jase, and to my gramps.

"Pleased to meet you all." She shook Gramps' hand. "You're the one who called."

Gramps nodded, and we all held up our brown-paper packages.

"Come in, come in." She grasped my hand and pulled me into the living room. "Stevie Rae Sanders." She looked into my face as if looking into my soul. "I wasn't sure if you were real or just a dream."

I blinked rapidly. "A dream?"

She laughed, and a delicate blue vein appeared in her throat. "Oh, yes. I dreamed you rode beside me on the bus coming home. I'd been to visit my best friend, Tonya Pauline. She lives in Amarillo. I caught the bus home the same day you said you caught a bus home from there. Isn't it strange? We may have passed each other in the station. Maybe that's why you seem so familiar."

I couldn't help it. I needed to sit down.

She must've seen my knees wobble. She took the painting from my nerveless grasp and led me to the sofa below the portrait of her mother.

"Your best friend lives in Amarillo?"

"Oh, yes. She just recently relocated there. She used to live right up the road in Flagstaff, near my older sister, Peg. I almost fainted when you told me why you were calling. I was right there in Amarillo, visiting Tonya for the first time. Right there in the same town where my father is buried. All those years he was there and I never even knew." Her hand went to her throat, covering the delicate blue vein.

Was her visit the catalyst for this whole thing? Coupled with my visit to Big Steve? I thought it very possible. There always seemed to be some cosmic coincidence, something that set the spirits in motion.

When I finally caught my breath, I reached toward the painting she still held in her hands. "Let's open these and let you see what your dad made for you."

She held it toward me and as I took it, an envelope fell to the floor. On the outside of the envelope a tiny lavender clown smiled up at us.

Jase looked at me as he bent to pick it up. When he handed it over, I could see the question in his eyes.

I gave him a slight shrug. I had no idea where the envelope

had come from, but I knew what it contained. Stormy Jensen had told me all about it on the bus.

"Your dad painted these paintings, and I know he wanted you to have them, but I don't want you to be disappointed . . . this one seemed to suffer some damage." I carefully peeled the paper away expecting to reveal the white blizzard blowing across the Barringer Meteor Crater.

But I got the surprise of my life when the paper fell away and the sad purple clown peered out. "Wow," I said. "It looks okay. I guess we were mistaken."

Stormy smiled and peeled off the rest of the paper. "Ohhh," her breath came out in a sigh. "It's amazing." Her fingers went to the painting and for a moment I was certain they would come away wet with paint. "He seems so sad," she said. And then she reached for the letter Jase held. "So this was wrapped up with the clown, huh?"

I nodded. "Apparently so, maybe my Aunt Sophia found it and put it in at the last minute. I've never actually—don't you want to see the other paintings first?"

She slid her finger beneath the envelope flap and pulled out folded sheets of lined paper. In a trembling voice she said, it's written to my mom, my sister, and me:

**My dearest Jean, my dearest daughters,**

**This prison life hasn't agreed with me. I've got a cough I can't shake. Cigarettes and painting are the only things keeping me sane.**

**I don't blame you for moving on with your life. I do wish I could've known my two girls. Just thinking of the three of you crushes me inside. I only wanted to give you the finest things, to make you feel special, important. Robbing the bank was wrong. I know that now.**

After I lost my job, I got desperate, couldn't make the house payment, the car payment, that big diamond ring . . . the bank just seemed like a thing not even connected with people. It seemed like the FDIC would replace the money and that it wouldn't hurt for me to have some to give to you. I just needed to not let you down, Jean. Instead, I wound up looking like a clown.

The prison psychologist thinks all my problems arose from my childhood. Ain't that a kick? He says people lose jobs all the time and they don't go rob banks. He thinks my psyche was irreparably damaged (or maybe he said my ego) when my father threw me out of the house when I was only twelve. Sink or swim, kid, he said. Sink or swim. What was I supposed to do? I swam. I think that killed my mother, too. She should have stood up for me but she wasn't strong. She died not too long after that.

Doc said that's why I panicked and robbed those banks, because I was afraid if you found out I couldn't make those payments, you'd throw me away the way Dad threw me away. But we were happy, you and I. We were happy, weren't we? I just wanted to preserve that happiness. Keep it going. So I did what I did.

I'm not using that as an excuse because it doesn't make anything right. I'm just telling you so you will know. So maybe you will explain it to my girls someday.

Jean, I don't know what is right anymore. The

shrink doesn't let me see my paperwork, but I sneaked a peek once when his back was turned. He labeled me a sociopath. How about that? First he tells me I'm damaged, and then he says I'm a sociopath. It means I'll never get out of here, but I'm not a bad person, Jean. I'm not. I was only confused. I love you and those girls. You all were the best things that ever happened to me.

That's why I'm putting these words in my paintings. Maybe someday my girls will know I did not desert them on purpose. I wouldn't do that to my children. It hurts too much.

All my love, now and forever, Jonny

For a moment the room was completely silent. And then I think we all heard it at the same time, the sound of water, dripping. I glanced around the room for a faucet but of course there was no faucet in the living room, and then I heard it again.

Jean, the woman in the painting, the lady-in-the-red-jacket, was crying. Tears trickled down her face and dripped off the frame, plopping one after the other onto the hardwood floor behind the couch. A few drops hit the back of the floral fabric, too. I could see darker spots in the cobalt colored petals of a giant blue hydrangea.

Stormy turned slowly. The painting hung directly behind her. "What on earth?" The tone of her voice said she must be dreaming. "How can this—"

I tried to distract her by ripping open another painting. "Here's my favorite," I nearly shouted. I held up the snowy scene of the horse pulling the sleigh. An arrow of sunlight shot through the front door glass, illuminating the shiny black horse and forward-facing driver.

"Oh," Stormy said. "So this is the one that was damaged . . ." She stood and took the painting from me and walked it closer to the light. "It looks like there's something under there. As if he painted over an older canvas. I've heard of artists doing that. Picasso, Van Gogh, probably many others . . ."

For the moment, the lady-in-red was forgotten.

As the sun went through the canvas, letters emerged as if through fog, or perhaps through lightly falling snow.

**LITTLE STORMY**

**I ALWAYS PICTURED US TAKING A RIDE IN THIS HAPPY SLEIGH**

**AT CHRISTMAS TIME**

Our new friend carefully leaned the painting against the front of the couch and her hand went to her throat again. "Oh, my . . ."

She picked up the lovely German shepherd portrait that reminded me of Jase's old ghost-hunting dog, Lady. "It's so beautiful."

Stormy ran her hand across it gently, and then she held the painting in front of the sunlight the way she'd done the other one. Spelled out beneath the layered paint:

**PEGGY JAY MY LITTLE DOLL
I OFTEN WONDER WHAT BECAME OF THE**

## BEAUTIFUL PUP
## I GOT YOU FOR YOUR SECOND BIRTHDAY

"That's my big sister, Peg." Stormy sighed. "She's disabled now, or she'd be here, too. She actually had our dad for a couple of years. The dog was named Callie. She lived a good, long, doggy life."

The lump in my throat threatened to suffocate me. We all looked back at the lavender clown. Was there another message hidden there?

Stormy picked it up and held the canvas up to the strong sunlight. Just as we suspected, a message appeared.

## MY DARLING JEAN
## I NEVER MEANT THINGS TO TURN OUT
## THIS WAY
## NO MATTER WHAT,
## I'LL ALWAYS BE YOUR CLOWN

Stormy's eyes clouded with tears. She clutched the painting to her breast. Behind her, the lady-in-the-red-jacket fell off the wall and hit the floor with a thud. The wind kicked up suddenly, battering the storm door and howling at the windows. The big wooden door slammed shut. It blocked out the sunlight and the living area was plunged into gloom. The temperature fell. A lacy rash of frost grew up the inside of the windowpanes.

Savage gusts of wind tore the gutters off the house and sent them flying across the yard. "What's happening?" Stormy cried.

The lights blinked on, then off, then on and off, on and off. "What is it?" Her voice was panicked. She closed her eyes and pressed her hands to the sides of her head.

I looked at Jase and he looked at me and even through the dimness I knew we were on the same wavelength.

Gramps might not have known exactly what was happening, but he had been around long enough he wasn't going to lose his cool over a little change in the weather. "Just hang on." He reached for Stormy's hand. "Sit here in this chair and we'll wait it out. Probably just a thunderstorm."

At that, the wind stopped. Everything grew eerily still.

Gramps yelled, "Duck and cover!" And then he yanked Stormy down and shielded her head as the windows imploded and glass went flying through the room in a deadly sideways rain.

We flattened ourselves on the floor, hands protecting the backs of our heads. Water splashed beneath our bodies. It seemed to be running out from under the couch. Jase wiped it from his face, brought his finger to his lips. "Salty." His tone was incredulous.

I slid my hand under the couch in search of the portrait. "I think it's tears," I said. "A lifetime of tears." I found the portrait, but the frame had broken away. Now, it was soggy photo paper, torn partway down the middle. I held it up. "Jase, *look*."

Jean's tears continued to flow. They had already washed away most of her second husband, the good-hearted policeman.

"We have to do something," Jase mouthed.

"But what?" I yelled. "What does she need? The clown?"
"Yes!" Jase's eyes were wild. "They have to be reunited somehow."

I crawled across the glass-littered floor and located the

lavender painting. It had landed on the couch, out of the swiftly flowing river of tears, but it sparkled with slivers of glass. I picked it up, not knowing what to do next.

The temperature dropped even more. Snowflakes fell like tiny feathers. Somewhere, a dog whined. The sound of sobbing shook the room.

I lay the soggy photo of the lady-in-red onto the solid lavender canvas of the clown. Something crackled and a giant black spot began to radiate away from the pictures in a circular fashion. The blackness obscured the couch, and began to eat up the beautiful hardwood floor.

"It's the meteor crater!"

Gramps and Stormy both had their eyes slitted against the cold and the possibility of more flying glass. Jase took my hand and pulled me away from what appeared to be a massive hole opening up beneath the mushy images. He dragged me backward just as the storm returned and lifted the roof right off the house.

Freight-train wind roared through the house. "Run!" I screamed.

The four of us scrambled into the narrow hallway leading toward the bedrooms. We hunkered together as sleet and snow swirled around our heads peppering our exposed arms and hands. Pieces of glass crunched beneath our bodies like ice.

The sound grew even more deafening. It vibrated the floor. The cyclone wind pulled at us, doing its best to break our holds on each other. For a moment my knees left the floor and I screamed and dug my fingers into Jase's flesh, holding on with all my might.

He smashed me down to the ground and threw himself across my back. Gramps draped his body over Stormy and we all clutched each other in desperation.

The wind ratcheted up another notch and I felt my hair pulled loose from its braid. The living room furniture slammed into the walls as chairs and end tables left the house and were sucked away through missing sections of roof. I glanced up just in time to see the huge, heavy sofa boosted into the air as if it were made of marshmallow fluff.

Green-hued daylight poured in with the icy snow and rain. The remaining strip of roof over the hallway lifted up on one corner. This is it, I thought. When this ceiling goes, we all go with it. Now I know why phantoms are reluctant to show themselves. The results can be catastrophic.

I heard roofing nails pop loose as shingles whirled through the air.

Just when I thought I couldn't hold on any longer, the storm ended as abruptly as it had begun. Ceiling tiles fell in on us as the remains of the furniture crashed back to earth.

I pushed at Jase's heavy body, realizing for the first time how hard it was to breathe. Coughing, I opened my eyes and glanced around. The air was nearly opaque with plaster dust and dirt from the yard.

"Is it over?"

Jase sat up, slapping at his hair and clothes. "I think so." He sat still, listening. In the distance, we could hear traffic far away, rushing down the Interstate.

"Gramps," I pushed at his leg as he rolled away from the younger woman. "Are you all right?" I'd been worried about him coming on this trip because we might have to sleep in a tent, on the ground. I hadn't worried about anything like this happening. Not in a million years.

He grunted, sitting up with effort. "I'm okay. Stormy?"

She groaned and rose onto her hands and knees. "You saved my life." She swiped at her clothing and dust rose in wings.

One by one we got to our feet. Unsteady, swaying, we

teetered down the hall, glancing upward at a swath of dark gray sky dotted with black clouds.

We peered around the edge of the door into the shambles that had been the living room. Everything was drenched and dripping. The roof was completely gone, two walls leaned toward each other precariously, and most of another wall had been pushed into the backyard.

"Holy cow," I said.

Jase let go a low whistle. "I've never seen anything like this. Is everyone positive they're all right?"

We all felt of our arms and legs and looked each other over for blood or bruises. "I think we're okay," I said. "Are you having any chest pain, Gramps?"

He grinned and patted his chest. "Nary a whimper. I guess if this didn't kill me, nothing will. When I get back home, I may even reapply for my old job at the P.D."

I couldn't help it. I rolled my eyes and blew air upward into my bangs. The man was incorrigible.

"Oh my God." Stormy Jensen's eyes mirrored the tone of her voice.

I followed her gaze to the one remaining, intact wall.

Somehow, the German shepherd painting and the horse pulling the sleigh were hanging side by side on the wall behind the place where the couch had been. Both paintings appeared untouched, as dry as unbuttered toast.

We all looked at the paintings and at each other.

Stormy Jensen's voice was a whisper. "What just happened?"

I tried to smile, almost made it. "Well, Stormy, I'd say that was your dad making certain you received your paintings." I'd also say you certainly lived up to your name. But I didn't say that, only thought it to myself.

She shook her head. "No. No. I don't believe in—I mean,

that was a storm. A freak storm." She walked closer to the edge of the foundation, where the front wall had stood. "Oh." Her voice held a note of awe. "We are the only house that was damaged. All the others on the block are fine, untouched."

The three of us moved to stand beside her.

I took her hand in one of mine while Jase took the other. I also grasped Gramps' hand so that we were all four connected. I closed my eyes. "Dear Lord, I believe these events are supernatural. I'm tired of denying the work of things we are too small to understand. Stormy's father obviously needed closure. Her mom did, too." I thought of the untouched paintings hanging on the one remaining wall. "Lord, if it be your will, please restore peace and harmony to this family the same way the paintings were restored to their place on the wall."

Jase muttered, "Amen." Gramps squeezed my hand. Stormy's grasp felt like a vise.

A breeze began to blow around the level of my knees. As it traveled upward, toward my face, it grew stronger and sweeter. The scent of honeysuckle permeated the air. I squeezed my eyelids tighter, afraid to open them and see what was happening.

This time the wind did not howl or whine; it simply enveloped us like a promise. When it lessened, I took a deep breath and hoped for the best.

Gramps said, "I smell honey."

"Honeysuckle," Stormy replied dreamily. "My mom's favorite flower. She had massive vines climbing the fence at our house when I was small."

I opened my eyes and glanced around. I was not too surprised to find the entire house back to normal except for the missing clown and the portrait of the lady-in-red.

Stormy turned slowly, one hand to her throat, mouth

slightly open. "Am I dreaming? Has this whole afternoon been nothing but a dream?" Her gaze went to the wall where the two new paintings were on display.

"Yes," Jase said. "Something like a dream." He reached over and picked up the folded letter, which lay unharmed on the coffee table, and handed it to Stormy.

She clutched it to her heart. "Can I visit him?" She asked. "At the prison cemetery?"

I hugged her shoulders. "I think he would love that. It's called Forever Field."

She looked at me without understanding.

"The place where he's buried," I explained. "It's behind the prison. Forever Field." I dug into the pocket of my jeans and pulled out the last remaining trinket from my time in Amarillo. "And when you go, please place this back on his tombstone." I dropped the smooth turquoise rock into her palm. "It was one of many clues that led us here."

She nodded and then her knees seemed to give way just like mine had done earlier. Jase and Gramps helped her to the couch while I surveyed the rest of the house, looking for damage. There was none.

"I wonder what happened to the clown," Stormy was saying when I reentered the living room. "I liked that painting."

Jase glanced up at me. "Yeah. I thought it was meant for you, but in the end, we never know what will happen."

She looked at him. "You mean this has happened before?"

Backtracking, Jase looked to me for help in covering his blunder.

"I think we should go look outside." I opened the door. "Maybe the painting got blown out . . ."

Gramps gave me the strangest look. Obviously the selective storm had been otherworldly. Nevertheless, he took Stormy's elbow and together we stepped outside into the mild air. There was nothing amiss in the yard. It was a typical end-of-summer, nearly-fall day.

"Arizona is gorgeous," Jase said. "But we're going to have to hit the road if we plan on seeing the Grand Canyon before it gets too late. Then we'll have to head on back. I don't want to lose my new job."

"Right," I agreed. "And I've got school-clothes shopping to do." I knew what Jase was doing. We had to get out of there, get back on the road home before Stormy could come to her senses and really begin to question us.

Gramps shook his head. "And the Widow Conner is probably pulling her hair out, wondering where I've got to."

We all laughed at that as we hugged Stormy and promised to keep in touch. I could see confusion lingering in her eyes, but behind that I also saw the beginnings of belief and even better, *relief*.

"How can I ever repay you for coming all this way?" She gripped my hand tightly.

"Just be happy," I said. "And make sure your sister gets her painting." I bit my lip. "Actually, there is one more thing you could do."

She smiled. Sometimes it makes people feel better to repay kindness with kindness. "Anything," she replied. "Anything at all."

"Could you write my dad? He's still in there. They let him keep one of your father's paintings in his cell. It's a pheasant in flight. I think it represented freedom to your father, probably mine as well."

"Of course I will. I have to tell him how thankful I am for his kindness." She hugged me again. "And for you." Holding my shoulders, she looked me in the eye. "Better than writing, I am going to visit your dad."

I nodded.

"I'll see him when I visit my own father in Forever Field."

"Thank you," I breathed. "I can't wait to write and tell him."

I hugged her again and then turned toward the El Camino where Jase and Gramps waited. It was a cozy vehicle, the three of us occupying one bench seat, but I didn't mind. After being away from them all summer, it was just what I needed to make me feel like myself again.

With a wave, I climbed into the passenger side, picked up Sarey, and scooted to the middle of the seat. Jase got in the driver's side and leaned over to give me a quick peck on the top of my head. Gramps slid in on my other side.

Snuggling Sarey on my lap, I waved goodbye to Stormy Jensen and, in essence, the Phantom of Forever.

Jase made a U-turn on her quiet, residential street, and I began to drag my fingers through my messy, unbraided hair.

Gramps settled himself more deeply into the leather seat and patted my knee. It was time to head back to Crossroads, Texas. Back to the place that would always be my home.


Next day:

Dear Diary,

Not only did we did get to see the Grand Canyon; we also got a quick view of Barringer's Crater.

Of course, we didn't have time to take the tour down into

the canyon, but simply standing at the lookout, searching for the so-called Phantom Ranch and gazing across the Painted Desert, made the entire trip even more special.

Gramps said he wanted us to start taking a weekend road trip every month. "There's too much we haven't seen." He chuckled when he said it, as if the things we had seen weren't on his list.

The Barringer Crater wasn't nearly as impressive as The

Grand Canyon, which was the most beautiful place I'd ever seen—all those colors and jagged peaks and valleys—and yet the Crater was memorable because it actually started to spit snow while we were there.

The three of us exchanged startled glances, and then we simply climbed back in the 'Camino and drove slowly away. It felt as if Jonny Jensen had just waved goodbye.

I slept a good portion of the trip home from Arizona. Gramps and Jase shared the driving—when one drove, the other slept. They didn't even wake me when we passed the sign about The Petrified Forest. Gramps said he figured it could wait for another day.

In a couple of years I will be taking my turn at the wheel, too. Maybe we'll come back this way again. But for this trip, I was thankful just to sleep with my head on Jase's shoulder, sometimes on Gramps', too.

We stopped at a K.O.A. campground late that evening and actually spent the night in our tents instead of in a teepee. I wasn't really worried about Gramps sleeping on the ground, or on his cot, anymore. Not after what we'd been through.

Unfortunately, we hadn't brought provisions for breakfast—although I would have loved frying bacon and eggs over a campfire—so in the next little town, we found a doughnut shop and loaded up on fried dough and coffee.

It was an amazing trip, Diary. But helping to reunite a couple of soul mate phantoms was not even the best part. After the Grand Canyon and the Barringer Crater, and after spending the night camping, we drove and drove, right on into the night.

The moon lit our path like a pearl-white beam all through the darkness. Jase and I both remarked on how it seemed to be celebrating us back together again. We held hands the whole way home. Gramps didn't even say anything.

But there I go, off on a tangent as usual. What I'm trying to say, Diary, is that when we drove up to our home in Crossroads, a man reclined on the front porch. It was dark remember? But we could see his shape in the moonlight. He'd pulled one of the chaise lounge chairs around front from the backyard, and he was stretched out in that chair like the king of all creation.

Even though he had an old straw cowboy hat covering his face, I knew from the shape of him it was Big Steve. Legs crossed at the ankles and one arm bent behind his head for a pillow, he appeared to be asleep.

None of us said a word as Jase pulled the 'Camino into the drive behind Gramps' old pickup. In a state of disbelief—like Stormy Jensen wondering if she was dreaming—I stepped out of the driver's side door behind Jase and stared across the top of the car. I wondered if I could be looking at a phantom. For a moment, my heart lurched in my chest.

If this was a phantom, then that would mean Big Steve was—

And then he sat up, lowering the cowboy hat with his free hand, and I was off and running toward him like an arrow shot from a bow.

He caught me easily, barely getting to his feet in time. I buried my face in his chest. "How'd you get here?"

He stroked my messy hair and whispered. "I took a bus. Just like you did when you came to see me and saved my life."

I clutched him around his middle and stepped back, tears salting my cheeks and lashes. "Daddy," I whispered, pulling him forward. "This is Jase. He's the one I told you about." I didn't let go of him. "Of course you already know Gramps. He's the other love of my life." Those words popped out. As usual, I examined them only after they'd already crossed my lips.

"Big Steve," Gramps said. He grasped my dad's upper arm and squeezed it solidly. "Welcome home. I'm sure one of the neighbors would have let you into the house. Seems like everyone has a key nowadays—since my stint in the hospital, that is."

My dad shook his head and looked down at me. "I've spent enough time indoors to last me forever. This old chair was the perfect place for me to wait. I knew you'd be home soon." He patted his shirt pocket. "Got your most recent letter right here."

Jase let go of my hand long enough to shake with Big Steve. "It's a pleasure to meet you, sir."

Big Steve grinned. "Thank you, Jase. It's a pleasure to be here."

And that's how I know I will never have to visit my Dad in Forever Field, Diary. After I started visiting him, he'd hired a new lawyer—with Aunt Sophia's help—who was able to get him out on parole because he'd proved himself to be a model prisoner. He never even told me he'd been taking college courses through the mail. Apparently, that goes a long way with a parole board.

Now he has come home to start a new life with us, as part of the family. But he refused to move in with Gramps and me. He said he didn't want to intrude.

"I appreciate what a wonderful life you created for my girl," he said to Gramps after we'd moved inside to the kitchen table that night. "I don't want to change a thing." He smiled at me and I could see why my mom had fallen in love with him. "But I'm not going away, I'll assure you of that."

(I think I exhaled when he said those words.)

"But I am going to Lubbock, just a couple of hours away." Here, he grinned and took my hand. "I've been accepted to the university, Stevie. I'm going to get my undergrad degree in

History, and then I will apply to the Texas Tech School of Law—"

I felt my eyes widen in surprise. "You're going to be a lawyer?" I thought it might be sort of a dark joke or something.

Big Steve nodded. "Sounds kind of ridiculous considering where I've spent the last few years, doesn't it?" He shook his head, looked at my hand, and then at the floor. "I've learned a lot. There are guys in there who had no chance, they had no family, no attorney to speak for them except those appointed by the court . . . and those were often so overworked it was like not having one at all." He smiled but it was a sad smile. "I made most of my own problems." His hand squeezed mine gently. "But that doesn't mean I can't turn over a new leaf."

I squeezed back.

"It's time I gave something back. Your mom would like that." He swallowed, hard. "I think about her all the time. Want to do something right for a change. Make her proud." His eyes sought mine. "And you, too, Stevie-girl. I think it's time you had a dad you don't have to be ashamed of."

"Oh," I said. "I never—"

He held up his hand. "I know, sweetie, I know." One side of his mouth went up in a grin. "You are just about the best human being I've ever met." He looked over at Gramps. "Your mom and grandparents did an amazing job with you." He swiped his free hand across his eyes. "And I'm not going to waste any more time feeling sorry for myself. We've got too much catching up to do, you and me. Too much living to get on with."

I was completely taken aback. Here he was in Crossroads, but already he was talking about leaving again. Moving two hours away. I gently pulled my hand back and stood up. I made my way to the kitchen window where Gran's old radio sat on the sill. It wasn't playing, but just being near it was like being near her. I needed her strength just then, her guidance.

"When will you move there?" I asked at last.

I heard a chair scrape the floor and I waited for someone's hand to grasp my shoulder. None did.

"I've just missed the fall semester," he said. "But that's all right. I've got to learn how to live in the world again before I can jump into college." He chuckled self-deprecatingly. "I'll aim for the spring semester, which begins in January."

I nodded. Touched the radio, ran water into a glass, took a sip. "So, where will you live until then?" I asked the question almost off-handedly. What I was really thinking was that he and Jase were both going to be moving to Lubbock, leaving me behind.

Gramps leaned back in his chair. "He'll stay with us, at least until he gets a job and gets on his feet—" He cut his eyes toward Big Steve. "And learns how to live in the world again."

Big Steve started to interrupt, but Gramps held up his hand. "I won't hear any arguments. You're family." He reached across the narrow kitchen space and tugged my braid (it had taken me an hour to detangle and re-braid it after the incident at Stormy's house and sleeping in the tent at the campground). "It just took a girl to help me remember that."

I leaned over and hugged Gramps around the neck.

My dad was swiping at his eyes again when I looked over at him. "Is that okay with you, Stevie-girl?" he asked.

I nodded. "Of course. I mean, I don't want to think about you—and Jase—moving off to Lubbock, but at least I won't have to worry about burying you out in Forever Field now." I wiped my own face; surprised my cheeks were damp, too. "And Lubbock really isn't that far, I guess."

Jase cleared his throat. "Who knows, maybe my mom and dad will let me stay here. I've got my license now, and a job. I can be independent. Stay in the house at least until it sells."

I met his gaze across the table. I knew he would do what was right, but if he could stay in Crossroads, I thought he'd do everything to make it happen.

Gramps made a little noise in his throat. "I'm just going to kick this out there, see what you all think about it."

We waited.

My grandfather seemed to be weighing his words. The kitchen was so quiet we could all hear the tick of the old Regulator clock on the wall, the hum of the Frigidaire in the corner. "Big Steve will be going off to Lubbock in a couple of months. I figure it will take that long for Jase's folks to get ready to move— if indeed they follow through on that—" He waited a beat, to see if everyone was listening. When he was certain everyone was focused, he continued, "I don't see why Jase can't take over the spare room when Big Steve goes on to Texas Tech." He leaned his chair back a little from the table. "If they don't want him to stay in the home place alone, that is."

Jase jumped out of his chair and stood in the middle of the room. "I could. I could do that. It would be great. Perfect. I— I don't want to go to a new high school and leave you and Stevie-girl." He looked at me, then at Gramps. "I wouldn't be any trouble in fact I would keep up the yard work and run errands and—"

Gramps and Big Steve glanced at each other. "You mostly do all that for me now." He looked at Jase kindly. "I'd be delighted if you'd stay with us." He set the front legs of his kitchen chair on the floor with a firm thud. "If your folks have no objections, of course."

Jase came to where I stood behind Gramps. He looped one arm around my shoulders and pulled me into his side. "I think they'll be okay with it, but considering my mom is already missing one son, I could be wrong."

I was happy Gramps had made the offer, but I was afraid

Jase was right. His mom wouldn't go off and leave him here. Her new house would be incredibly empty. First Rusty, then Jase? She would probably lose her mind.

Peering up at him, I could see that Jase knew it, too. There was a deep sadness in his eyes that hadn't been there moments earlier when he'd jumped up out of his chair. It was one of those second-thought expressions I was learning to recognize.

I was beginning to think we'd never learn what happened to Rusty. It was sort of like watching a nightmare unfold bit-by-bit, day-by-day, night-by-night.

After all that planning, and Jase's common-sense pronouncement, we all seemed deflated. We sat around the table snacking and drinking iced tea and chocolate milk while Jase told Big Steve all about his brother, Rusty.

Then we went on to tell him about the experience with Stormy Jensen, and I made myself a mental note to write her a letter, to let her know Big Steve wouldn't be there when she went to visit her own father in Forever Field.

Big Steve didn't seem the least bit surprised by our supernatural experiences. Of course he is the one who started it by asking me to go out to visit Jonny Jensen in the first place. "I told your mom about this, Stevie, but you were too small to know."

I looked at him expectantly. The tops of my ears actually felt hot, as if in expectation of something profound.

He shifted his weight in the chair, stretched his long legs out to the side of the table, took a long drink of tea, and finally said,

"Your other Gram, my mom." He stopped, and then shrugged as if giving himself permission to continue. "She had the gift, too."

I watched his face for a hint of a smile or some further explanation. When none was forthcoming, Jase took the bit in his teeth.

"The gift? You mean, like Stevie, able to communicate with

spirits?"

Big Steve nodded. "Yes. She was also able to know things before they happened. She tried to warn me about drinking and driving. Told me, and rightly so, that it wasn't me who would suffer the consequences but my loved ones." He cleared his throat. "I don't think it's a coincidence that your mom was killed by a drunk driver while she was out searching for a drunken me, do you?"

I didn't want to say it aloud, but I was a little skeptical. Everyone knows if you drink and drive something bad will happen, right? As much as I wanted to have a psychic connection (so to speak) with the paternal grandmother I'd never met, I wasn't convinced this was it. Besides, I didn't have second sight, like she did, knowing things that hadn't happened yet. I just had some sort of magnetic appeal for spirits. Jase, too, I think. After all, he was the one who had first encountered the phantom pilot. On the other hand, maybe if he hadn't found me at the Taylor place, he wouldn't have been able to help the pilot after all. I'd never thought of that.

Diary, it boggles my brain if I let it, how all these things seemed connected in retrospect. But at that moment, Big Steve seemed to be waiting on some sort of acknowledgement of his theory.

"She sounds amazing," I said. "So many supernatural things have happened to me and Jase, and now Gramps, that I am a total believer. I have absolutely no doubt that Shakespeare was right and there are more things in Heaven and Earth than can possibly be dreamt of in our philosophy."

Big Steve nodded. "Or as William Blake wrote, 'To see a world in a grain of sand, and a Heaven in a wildflower. To hold infinity in the palm of your hand, and eternity in an hour . . .'"

I don't know if my face showed it, but I was momentarily dumbfounded. To hear my father quoting poetry; my father whom I'd never thought of as anything except that guy who deserted us, or lately, as that guy in prison, well, it was quite the eye-opener.

"That's a long poem," I said. "I don't think I really understand it.

Big Steve grinned. "Me, either. I think it's just about how all things are connected through God." He laughed goodnaturedly. "Don't look so shocked. I've had a few years to do little more than read and make license plates."

I felt my cheeks burn. "Sorry," I said. "Was it that obvious?" He reached across the table and clasped my hands in both of his. "I'm used to it, honey." His gaze went to Gramps' face. "That's what we were joking about having to learn to live in the real world again. No more lying around reading poetry all day."

I wasn't certain if he was serious, or not. His tone seemed joking, but his expression didn't quite match. I just squeezed his fingers and pretended to understand. No matter what, I was simply glad he was here. Glad I had a father after all. Having one that could quote William Blake was pretty cool, too.

Big Steve stood and stretched. "First thing tomorrow morning, I'll be starting the job search." He looked down at me. "One other thing I learned in addition to taking the college courses while I was in there . . . I also gained some skills in offset printing."

I saw Gramps' head come up. "Is that right?"

My dad nodded. "I'm going to check on the Crossroads newspaper, see if they need help, but since it's only once a week, I may have to go to one of the larger towns in the area."

"You should check Lubbock," I blurted. "The Avalanche

Journal is a big paper and since you'll be going to Tech soon—"

"That's good thinking, kiddo," he replied. "Very good thinking. And even if I do go to work there, it's not so far away that I can't drive back and forth for a while."

I nodded. It could be the perfect solution.


Saturday


What a wild week. School is so different this year. I have almost every class with Jase. We picked our schedules together last year, so I hoped it would be this way, but still, we weren't sure we'd get all our first choices. It was a nice surprise.

He picks me up in the morning and sometimes comes in and has breakfast with us. I still love the way he just opens the back door and walks right in. Seems like he's been a member of the family since day one.

The only difference in our schedules this year is that Jase is still in track and I'm stuck in plain old PE. I hate PE.

Jase says his track may be only temporary. He practices before school, at six a.m., and then he showers and picks me up at eight. It's a tough schedule. Especially since he still works at Skinny's after school. I don't see how he does it.

But since today is Saturday and there aren't any track meets yet—the first one is in two weeks—Jase and I have decided to get together with Billy Bob and Derol. We're going to ride Buddy and clean out his stall.

Of course you know what they say about the best laid plans of mice and men . . . Jase came in the back door about ten o'clock. He didn't even call first.

I was sitting in front of the TV with a bowl of Alpha Bits cereal watching American Bandstand. Gramps was outside in the back yard looking at the old AC unit. The temperature was still in the nineties even though it was September.

When I saw the look on Jase's face, well, I couldn't tell what it meant. I'd never seen that particular expression before. Not on him.

I jumped up almost spilling my cereal. "What is it? What's wrong?"

He sat down on the couch and stared at the TV.

I set my bowl on the coffee table and sat beside him. "What is it? Another letter from Rusty?" I said a tiny silent prayer that's what it was.

Jase shook his head. "No." Then he glanced at me. "I wish it was." He clasped his hands between his knees and sort of leaned forward. I'd seen older men do that when they were thinking about something. It was sort of universal.

"Jase, you're scaring me—"

He sat back. "Sorry. Didn't mean to. It's just, well. Mom says she isn't moving to Lubbock no matter what. She says this is our home and Rusty's home and when he comes back she wants to make sure she is right here waiting for him."

"Oh." That isn't at all what I expected to hear. "Is that bad?" Jase shook his head. "My folks had a big argument about it."

He closed his eyes. "They don't fight. Ever. They seldom even disagree."

I could see the pain in his expression now. That's what it was. Pain.

"Dad says it's his job and he doesn't have any choice. Mom says he will have to go without her."

I didn't know what to say. "What do you think will happen?"

Jase shrugged. "Dad said he would try driving back and forth but you know that's a two hour trip both ways. Four hours every day." He reached over and straightened a doily on the coffee table. "I know Big Steve said he would try it if necessary, but that would be temporary. Not like this." He looked up at me. "I like to drive but that's asking a lot in my opinion."

I nodded. I thought so, too. But I knew Jase's mom. She wasn't the selfish type, so it certainly wasn't because she just wanted her way. Then it occurred to me that Jase's problem would be solved if she stayed. "Well, at least you could stay here with her."

Voice so low I could barely hear him, Jase said, "Yeah. At least there's that."

Just then Gramps came in from the back yard. "Well hello, Jason Lee." His voice was jovial, but he must have felt the tension in the air. He stopped and looked at us more closely. "Why the long faces?"

I explained what had happened and he sat down in his recliner and rubbed one hand across the top of his balding head. "I wouldn't worry too much about it," he said. "These things have a way of working themselves out."

And you know what, Diary? He was right. As usual. After a couple of days of negotiations, Mr. Lee's employer offered him a company car and a fuel allowance so he could drive back and forth until they decided whether or not they really wanted to move.

"It's a temporary solution," Jase said, echoing what he'd mentioned earlier about Big Steve. "But Mom is convinced that Rusty is going to come home any day now so she's happy with it." A small smile played across his lips. "And Dad is kind of excited about having a company car. I think after being told he had to move or else, this softened the blow."

"Our prayers have been answered. Maybe not in the exact way we thought they would but—"

Jase took my hand. "You've been praying, too?" I nodded.

"Always."

His smile turned into a full-blown grin as he squeezed my fingers, then reached across and took my other hand, too. He closed his eyes and said, "Dear Lord, thank you for these answered prayers. And Lord, thank you for bringing back this girl, my best friend in the whole world, my Stevie-girl." His voice fell to a whisper. "Amen."

When he said "Amen," Diary, chills coated my arms and legs. I echoed his amen, and I was going to add my own thanks as well, but just then the front door opened and Big Steve walked in. His grin was every bit as broad as Jase's.

"I got it," he said. "I got the job, Stevie-girl." His voice was filled with pride. He had been in Lubbock talking to the lead printer at the Avalanche Journal.

Jase and I both jumped up off the couch. I rushed into Big Steve's arms, which he held wide open. He caught me and swung me in a little circle.

"That's great news!" I said.

Jase patted him on the back and I thought I heard him murmur. "Thank you, God, for more answered prayers."

And Diary . . . that statement of thanks meant more to me than almost anything. When Big Steve turned me loose, he grabbed Jase's hand and gave it a firm shake. "You kids are something else. I've already looked at a couple of apartments in Lubbock, and I want both of you to come up and give me your opinion." He pulled me to his side. "Both of them have an extra bedroom for you, Stevie-girl. It will be your home away from home." He looked at Jase. "And there will always be a place for you, too, Jase. It's obvious you are a big part of this family."

We both hugged him, then, and I felt a loosening sensation in my chest. For the first time since my Gramps' heart attack last year, I began to breathe easily again. Strange how things work out. If Gramps hadn't had a heart attack, he might never have given me the box of letters from Big Steve, the ones he'd kept hidden from me all those years. The ones that became the catalyst for my trip to Forever Field and the Amarillo prison.

I would never say this out loud, but I have found myself wondering . . . if Gramps hadn't had a heart attack, if he hadn't given me the letters that let me know Big Steve was in prison, if I hadn't taken the bus up there to see him, if we hadn't reconnected . . . would Big Steve have gone to the trouble to get a new lawyer who eventually got him paroled?

I'll probably never ask him, but I will always wonder.

On the other hand, perhaps all the things that happened were just God's way of getting me up there to connect with the lady-in-the-red-jacket. Apparently people who can communicate with spirits are not that common.

The fact that Jase and I found each other because of this ability, and that my Gramps got caught up in it, too, those things seem as supernatural as the spirits themselves. And why can't God and religion be thought of as supernatural? Seriously, how can it be thought of as anything else? How cool is it that my own grandmother—the one I never met—also had the ability to see things, to know things.

I'm once again reminded of that Shakespeare quote I like so much, "There are more things in Heaven and Earth than can possibly be dreamt of in our philosophy."

I can tell you one thing on this earth, Diary. My life has grown better and better with the addition of Big Steve. He's funny, and loving, and he reads everything and anything that crosses his path. Just like me.

Oh, the conversations we have. Amazing. And when Jase and Gramps are here, things really get lively. Of course I don't see Big Steve all that much. He works the night shift in the printing department of the Lubbock Avalanche Journal.

Maybe that's a good thing. It means we sort of see each

other coming and going. And on his days off. That means we are getting to know each other gradually, a little at a time.

It all worked out perfectly for him since he is going to take classes at Texas Tech during the day. I was sort of proud that he'd learned offset printing in prison. As he said, being locked up causes a person to either grab hold and take advantage of the time to learn or give up and disintegrate into a world of self-pity. Yep. I really admired him for that. Still, I have to wonder (again), what if he hadn't got drunk and went to prison at all? Where would he have been now? Would he still be an angry alcoholic without a job, or would he have found a better path?

As far as that goes, would the three of us—him, Mom, me— still be a little family in another town, without my Gramps?

It's too much for my pointed head to figure out. If Big Steve hadn't taken off, deserted Mom and me then got arrested and sent to prison . . . I never would have moved here and found Jase.

From this side of events, it seems that everything has worked out the way it should. Except for losing my Mom and my Gran, of course. Nothing was right about losing them so early.

We also have the missing puzzle piece that is Rusty. And Diary, it is such a huge part of Jase and his family. It's like negative space, that thing we learned about in Art class—you know, the way you surround the subject of the painting with blank canvas to draw more attention to it?

But Diary, here's the part that really blows my mind. Jase has joined the ROTC at school. Reserve Officer Training Corps. My Jase. My sweet, literary Jase, my writer. The one who would rather pick up an ant and write a short story about it instead of crushing it under his heel. The one who is so gentle and good that in all the time I've known him, I've never known him to have an enemy. The one who loves animals almost as much as me.

That Jase.

He's learning to use a gun. Learning to lead others into battle. Learning battle techniques.

He won't say for certain, Diary, but I suspect I know what he's thinking. And I don't like it. I'm afraid he's got it in his head that he's going to join the military when he gets out of school. That he's going to go to Vietnam to search for Rusty himself. I haven't come right out and asked him, but I'm pretty sure that's what he has in mind. After all, he's that kind of guy.

And you know what, Diary? It's given me an idea, too. It wasn't just Jase; it was a combination of him and Big Steve. I've decided I'm going to Vietnam, too. I thought about being a journalist—nonfiction writer that is—so my next elective in school will be Journalism.

I won't be as good at creative writing as Jase, but I'll kill 'em on the research part. I can easily see myself in a foreign country with a pen in one hand and a notebook in the other digging for the facts of a story. I might have to write about someone like the POW who blinked in Morse code. I could write articles for *Time*. For *Life*. Maybe even for *Reader's Digest*.

It makes sense, doesn't it? One more of those puzzle pieces falling into place. Big Steve working for the newspaper, taking classes at Tech; Jase planning to search for his brother in Vietnam, and me getting a new idea about a way to use my love of research. It just makes sense.

Except for the part about my life-long idea that I wanted to be a doctor. Maybe I need to give this some more thought.

Whatever happens, I feel like it's only a matter of time before we solve the mystery together. The mystery of Rusty.

On the other hand, I pray this stupid war will be over before we can put any of our half-formed plans into action. I pray—

daily—that it will be a bad memory by the time Jase gets old enough to go.

It's easy to think of him traveling the country in the El Camino, sleeping in roadside parks and picking apples in Wisconsin like Jack Kerouac or John Steinbeck, but I can't bear the thought of him carrying a rifle over his head while crossing a rain swollen river in a jungle eight thousand miles away.

More than anything, Diary, I pray to the Lord every single day and every single night to please, please, please let Rusty come home like he let Big Steve come home. But you know what? I'm not sure I'm asking God in the proper way. I haven't had a lot of instruction in praying. I've just always talked to God like I talk to myself.

Should I ask God to let Rusty come home (that sounds like God is keeping him from returning, doesn't it?), or should I say please HELP Rusty get home? Or should I just pray that Rusty's captors release him unharmed? As far as that goes, maybe I should be praying that he is still alive at all.

I know. I'm overthinking the whole thing like I always do.

I can't help it. I just worry about everything. But one thing I know . . . miracles do happen. One happened for Big Steve and me. And one happened for Stormy Jensen and her sister. So maybe that's what I should pray for.

I will pray for one more miracle.

I will pray for the war to be over and for Rusty to come home safe and sound with all the other prisoners of war and all those like him that are listed as missing in action.

I will pray it every day. It can't hurt.

# EPILOGUE

Jᴀsᴇ's Dᴀᴅ ᴅʀᴏᴠᴇ ʙᴀᴄᴋ ᴀɴᴅ ꜰᴏʀᴛʜ ᴛᴏ Lᴜʙʙᴏᴄᴋ ꜰᴏʀ ᴛʜᴇ rest of the year. His mom began to fill in those new blank spaces where her husband used to be. She actually went back to her Women's Bible Study Group and she began to volunteer at the local hospital.

"I feel bad not being there for her," Jase told me one Saturday at Skinny's station. "It seems like I'm not home very much with work and school—"

"And me," I said.

Jase just smiled. "But on the other hand, she seems to be getting out more and doing things on her own again."

I remember thinking that was a good thing. And then, around Christmas, the owner of our local lumber store got really sick and decided to cut down on his hours at work.

Mr. Lee was offered the position of general manager. Needless to say, he jumped at the chance to move back to Crossroads and his family.

Funny how things work out, isn't it?

Of course, Big Steve had a lot of compromising to do in his new job. At first he found it very difficult to work at night and take classes during the day. After spending only a few days with us, he got approved for his apartment and moved on to Lubbock. I talked to Aunt Sophia on the phone a couple of times and she said all the thanks for him getting out of prison should go to me.

I argued with her, of course, but she said if I hadn't visited when I did, she didn't think he would have even bothered to try for a new attorney. She never mentioned it, but I just wonder how much money she loaned him to get that lawyer. I also wonder how she ever got Uncle Burney to agree.

That's what family is for, according to Gramps, but I don't know. It sure seems hard on everyone else when one person runs afoul of the law. I would never say that, though. After all, I'm still a kid. There's a lot of stuff I don't know.

Big Steve hung the painting of the Pheasant in Flight on the living room wall in his new apartment. I could tell how much it meant to him. That's why I was so surprised the next time I went to visit him and the painting was no longer there.

He saw me looking at the spot where it had hung. "Gone, baby girl." He chuckled to himself. "I wouldn't tell this to just anyone, but I know you'll understand." He walked over to the window behind the kitchen sink.

For a few moments, I thought he'd forgotten about me.

Then he said, "I left the window open, that first night I was here." His shoulders were bunched up tight beneath his chambray shirt.

I waited for him to turn around, to explain.

When he didn't, I couldn't stand it any longer. "What happened?" My voice came out a bit shrill.

Big Steve touched the window sash. "It flew away." He leaned forward, looked outside as if he might spot the bird on the wing. A sad chuckle escaped him. "I can't much stand to be in a place with all the doors and windows locked." He cleared his throat. "When I got up the next morning, the bird was gone."

"You mean the whole painting? Gone? Maybe someone stole it." I didn't know why I would try to justify it after all the things I'd seen, but there you go. Denial is not just a river in Egypt.

Big Steve didn't respond. He simply turned and walked into his bedroom. I heard the closet door open and close, and then he came back holding what appeared to be the painting.

He held it up for me to examine. The sky above the stream was empty except for a few clouds.

"The pheasant flew?"

My dad nodded. "It's free now." He shrugged. "Thanks to you, and Jase, and your Gramps. I think Jonny finally found his wings."

It's been a while now, Diary, and I'm still reflecting on that strange summer. Forever Field will live in my memory, well, forever. But I have to wonder if there is any way Jonny Jensen can possibly know the effect his life has had on us, on my little family.

That's another thing I think about sometimes . . . his life seemed so empty after he robbed those banks. As empty as the sky over the lake.

He lost his wife and his children, and spent his entire life encased in loneliness and yet, because of his paintings, and the lady-in-the-red-jacket, Big Steve got a second chance at a family. And so did I.

But to really examine it, I'd have to go back to Crybaby Bridge. That's where Jase and I were when Gramps had his heart attack. We were trying to solve the mystery of the crying baby.

Once again, it amazes me the way things work out. It's one of our new favorite topics, Jase and me. We keep hoping all these things are somehow leading up to bringing Rusty home. That would be the icing on the cake.

Jase says it will happen.

I'm beginning to believe him.

My newest question is this . . . will our lives always revolve around solving mysteries for phantoms? Like the one that keeps appearing beside the highway between Crossroads and Lubbock?

Big Steve mentioned it the first time Jase and I made plans to visit him for the weekend. "Be sure to watch out for that odd hitchhiker just after sunset," he said one day. "She's awfully pale. Don't even think about stopping. I asked someone at the paper about her and he said they call her See-through Stella. He said legend has it she was killed by a hit and run driver after she had an argument with her mom and tried to run away. That's why she was out on the highway. Legend also says if you pick her up, she'll ride along with you for a while, but when you stop to let her out . . . she's no longer there."

"See-through Stella? Sort of an old fashioned name. Probably happened a while ago." I tucked the tip of my braid between my lips. "Sounds like she's trying to get back home, doesn't it? I'd better do some research. I have a distinct feeling we may soon be getting better acquainted."

Big Steve raised one eyebrow but he didn't disagree. I think things are about to get very interesting around here. Again.

# ABOUT THE AUTHOR

Ann Swann was born in the small West Texas town of Lamesa. She grew up much like Stevie-girl in *The Phantom* books, though she never got up the nerve to enter the haunted house. Before becoming a writer, Ann did everything from answering 911 Emergency calls to scheduling commercials in a rock-n-roll radio station to teaching elementary school. She still lives in Texas with her husband, Dude, and two rescue cats, Oscar and Mojo. When she's not writing, Ann is reading. Her to-be-read list has grown so large it has taken on a life of its own. She calls it Herman.